THE CAESAR'S SECRET
BOOK 2

AN ADVENTURE GUILD STORY

ERNEST DEMPSEY
CHANDLER DEMPSEY

1

ROME, PRESENT DAY

"We can't just leave it here," Diego said. "What if someone comes in and finds it?"

Diego had always been the cautious one. Never one to take unnecessary risks, he didn't think his sister's plan was smart.

"Like who?" Corin asked. "The cleaning ladies?"

"Oh, I don't know. What about those two guys who tried to steal it from us?"

Desmond finished lacing his shoes at the desk a few feet away and shook his head. "You worry too much. Anyone ever told you that?"

Diego glared at him.

Corin covered her mouth to mute the chuckle she couldn't stop from erupting.

"I'm just saying this is an ancient artifact. It's potentially priceless. Do you really want to risk leaving it here for someone...anyone...to find and take?"

"Yeah, but it's added weight," Corin said. She was always one for efficiency. Maybe it came from her deep interest in math and science. "We need to be able to move fast if we run into those guys again."

"Come on," Desmond protested. "What are the odds we bump into them again?"

Diego crossed his arms and gave his best chastising frown. "If they managed to find us here at the hotel, know what room we were in, and follow us to the temple where we found this thing, I'd say there's a good chance we could see them again."

"Fine," Corin said. "I'll carry the thing."

She looked down at the stone fragment on the desk. It was lying on top of a map they'd discovered in the museum at the Ellerbys' latest exhibit. The three kids had followed the clues to an ancient temple located on the other side of the city. To get there, they'd had to ditch their bodyguard, Sam, along with keeping their activities secret from the Ellerbys.

They'd thought for sure their little secret would be uncovered when they came home the previous night. The room had been ransacked by the two British men who were trying to steal the map and, soon after, the tablet. Luck had been on their side, and they managed to get in their beds mere moments before Sam and Desmond's parents walked in the room.

"No, you don't have to do that," Diego said. "I'll carry it. It was my idea not to leave it here."

"Okay," Corin said, "that's fair."

"We should probably make a paper copy, you know, just in case."

"Good idea," Desmond agreed. He stepped over to the desk and rummaged through the center drawer, finding a piece of paper and pen. He quickly scribbled down the Latin letters and when he was done carefully folded it and stuffed it in his back pocket.

"I sure hate taking this map," Diego said as he gently rolled the ancient paper up and slid it into a plastic sleeve he'd retrieved from the gift shop downstairs.

"Just don't damage it," Desmond warned. "No map. No more clues. No more clues means no treasure."

The pressure of his statement weighed on Diego. He knew what was at stake. "You know what? I have an idea."

He took the map and tucked it into the gift bag he'd brought from the shop. Then he placed the stone tablet in his backpack and slung it over his shoulders.

"What's the idea?" Corin wondered.

"We're going to put this stuff in Desmond's parents' room."

Shock hit both Corin and Desmond.

"Wait. What?" Desmond wasn't sure he'd heard correctly, and if he had, he clearly didn't like the idea. "Did I hear you say what I thought you said?"

"It's the only place where those guys won't look," Diego explained. "Think about it. They were following us, not your parents. If they do come back, however unlikely that might be, I doubt they would check their room. They probably don't even know what room your parents are staying in."

Desmond raised an eyebrow as he considered the idea.

"I don't like it," Corin said, suddenly the one concerned about risk taking. "What if they look through your stuff? And what excuse are you going to give them?"

"They won't know," Diego said. He motioned to the closet.

The other two frowned, not understanding.

Diego paced over to the closet door and flung it open. He pointed down at the black fireproof box sitting on the floor. The object was about two feet tall and easily that wide.

"A safe?" Corin asked.

"Yep. We put this stuff in his parents' safe. That way, they won't even know it's there."

"What if they're using the safe and already have stuff in it?"

Diego chuckled and offered his own frown in return. "No one uses those things, do they?"

Corin rolled her shoulders. She had no context for an answer. She and her stepbrother hadn't traveled much in their short lives, not outside the country, anyway.

"I haven't seen my parents use those before," Desmond offered. "It just might work, and it looks like the map and the stone will fit inside."

"Exactly," Diego said. "Then we just have to take the paper you put in your pocket to that priest and ask him what it says. That way, these things will be safe, and I don't have to lug them around worrying about damaging them."

"Why don't we just use that safe?" Corin asked. "Seems logical."

She stepped into the closet and tried to move the thing. It was bolted to the floor. "See? They couldn't take this without making a lot of noise or causing a scene."

"I just want to be extra careful, okay?" Diego pleaded. "I know the safe is...um, safe, but putting it in his parents' room will make it even—"

"Safer?" Desmond said with a smile.

"Yeah." Diego blushed.

"Fine," Corin relented. "Can we just put this stuff away and get moving? The sooner we get to the church, the sooner we can figure out where this thing is telling us to go next."

She walked over to the door and grabbed her backpack from the floor. She'd already stuffed two water bottles and an energy bar in there in case she got hungry. The others had prepared similarly, putting a few simple supplies in their bags to get them through the day. They had a little money, too, so they could stop at a bakery and get some bread and cheese if they needed to.

"You guys ready?" Corin asked, putting her hand on the door latch.

The boys nodded.

"All right then. Let's do this." She pulled down on the latch and yanked the door open.

Standing there in the hallway, just beyond the threshold, was a familiar face.

Corin stared up at the man with surprise. She blinked but probably didn't realize how fast she was doing it.

She swallowed hard and absently took a step back from the menacing figure blocking her path.

"Sorry," she said. "I didn't know you were there."

She felt her hands brush against the boys behind her and realized she'd backed into them.

The man offered a toothy, wicked grin. "Going somewhere?"

2

R ome

DESMOND STEPPED in front of Corin, putting himself between her and the big man in the black suit. "What are you doing here so early, Sam?" Desmond almost sounded demanding and then cleared his throat to make a sort of apology for any hint of disrespect.

Sam was their...caretaker? Babysitter? Bodyguard? To the three kids, it felt like the middle answer. They'd managed to slip free of his grasp at the museum gala celebrating the Ellerbys' discovery. Then, later, they got away from him again to visit the temple where they found the first fragment. The clue on the map called it a key, according to the priest, and apparently there were three of them.

With one-third of their journey complete, the kids were well on their way to making the discovery of a lifetime: an ancient treasure, hidden long ago by some important or wealthy person. Julius Caesar, it seemed, had also been seeking the same treasure when he was captured by pirates in a story that had become legend down through the centuries.

Sam stepped into the room and crossed his arms. "What am I doing here so early? It's my job to protect you." He looked beyond Desmond to the other two. "All of you. Which means I am going to keep a close eye on you. All. Day. Long. And for the rest of this trip."

"Sounds like a boring gig," Corin chirped.

Diego slugged her in the arm without looking. She winced but said nothing, not even "ouch." Instead, she snorted at her own joke.

"It *is* a boring gig," Sam said. "And the more boring it is, the better. The last thing I need is to be chasing you three all over the city."

"Yeah, but I doubt my parents would want us to stay cooped up in here all day," Desmond argued. "They brought us here so we could see the sights and learn stuff about history."

"Leaving *my* sight isn't what they had in mind. And your parents aren't here now."

"They aren't?" Desmond frowned. "Where did they..." He knew the answer before he finished the question. They'd already be at the museum or doing interviews for an Italian paper or something.

"No, they aren't here. Which means you're in my care all day. I've also brought Billy along to help make sure none of you slippery kids get out of our view again."

Billy, the other security guard that worked for the Ellerbys during daylight hours, stepped into the doorway. He also had a stern look on his face and crossed his arms to make himself look more imposing.

"If you don't let us take a look around the city, my parents won't be happy."

Sam knew that would be their argument. He deserved better than this. He'd worked private security for wealthy brats before. The Ellerbys were a nice couple, generous and understanding. They trusted Sam and his team implicitly. He knew there was no way they'd be okay with him locking their child and his friends up in a hotel room for the duration of the day.

He knew Mrs. Ellerby would be especially annoyed at the idea. Over the years, he'd witnessed her encouraging Desmond to get outside more, to explore the world. No, keeping them in a small room wouldn't do. Which is why he'd brought Billy along for backup.

The mere notion that he'd need another adult male to help babysit these three kids was irritating to say the least. He'd been trained to protect adults, to take down bad people in ways these kids couldn't imagine. But somehow, these kids had managed to outfox his expertise and sneak off to do who knew what. He counted himself lucky that none of them were hurt or lost somewhere in the vast city of Rome. Sam didn't want to count on luck again, thus his backup standing in the doorway.

"Today is your lucky day," Sam said with a broad grin. The expression told the three kids they weren't going to like what followed. His tone was overly condescending as he spoke in an almost baby-talk voice. "Billy and I will be giving you a guided tour. We've already gone over some really neat spots with your parents. They had lots of good suggestions. So, for the rest of your stay here in Italy, my friend Billy here"—he put his hand over his shoulder to point at the second bodyguard—"and I will be with you the entire time. When you need to eat, we'll eat with you. When you need to have a drink, we'll be there."

"You guys are *not* going to the bathroom with me," Corin stated.

Sam paused for a moment. An uncomfortable look crossed his face, and he cocked his head to the side to look up at the ceiling. "Okay, no. I will not...we will not be going to the bathroom with you."

"Or us," Desmond said. "I need my privacy."

"Yeah, me too," Diego added.

"Okay, fine. We aren't going to the bathroom with any of you. But we'll be waiting just outside when you need to go."

The kids almost giggled at Sam's abrupt change from a commanding to a now awkward tone. They'd didn't laugh, though, because they knew that any plans they'd made and any ideas they might have had about figuring out the next clue to the map had just been flushed down the drain.

Unless they could figure out another way to get away from these two. Perhaps they would just need to be patient until the moment presented itself.

"Cool," Desmond said. "Where are we going first?"

Sam's irritation dissipated, and he forced an appeasing grin back onto his face. "We'll be getting you three something to eat first. Your parents have given me the money we need for the day, so you won't need to take anything with you."

He motioned to the backpacks. "Those can stay here."

Diego turned and looked at Corin, who was looking to Desmond for an answer.

"Thanks," Desmond said, "but we prefer to take them with us if that's okay with you. Wouldn't want anything to happen to our stuff if someone were to...I don't know, break into this room."

Sam tilted his head back, glaring down at the boy over his lower eyelids. "That brings me to my next point." He took a step forward. "I saw what happened in here yesterday. Don't for a second think I'm stupid. I know what you three are up to."

"You...you do?" Diego stuttered, fear wrapped around his voice and causing it to crackle.

"Oh yes. You think you can just run amok all over the city, doing whatever you want. But I'm not stupid." He made a fork with two fingers, pointed them at his eyes, and then pointed them at Desmond. For all his bravado, Sam didn't know what they were doing. He didn't have a clue about the map or the stone tablet in Diego's bag.

"So," Sam went on, "we'll be storing your things in your parents' room for safekeeping while we are out seeing the sights and doing the things that good little tourists do."

The three kids fought hard to keep back the laughter.

"Okay," Desmond said after a moment of struggling. He did his best to sound dejected. "If you think that's best, Sam."

"Oh, I do. And there is one more thing you're going to need to do for me."

"Which is?"

"No more lies."

Desmond looked offended.

Diego remained stoic, while Corin crossed her arms in a defensive posture.

"What do you mean, no more lies?" Desmond asked. "What have we lied about?"

"Oh, I don't know...everything?" The big bodyguard put his hands out wide, like the room they were standing in was covered in lies. "The museum, your disappearance, whatever happened to this room, the three of you going missing for hours on end—you lied about all of it to me and your parents."

"Okay," Corin defended, "first of all, we didn't lie. We were honest about everything...for the most part. I mean, it's all about presentation."

Sam shook his head. "No, from now on you three tell the truth about everything. Do you understand?"

"So," Diego said, suddenly finding a drop of courage, "if we somehow manage to get into some kind of trouble, you want us to tell Desmond's parents about it? I mean, that would get you in trouble, too, wouldn't it?"

Sam grumbled. "That's the whole idea of us watching over the three of you like hawks for the rest of this little vacation. You won't be getting into any trouble."

"Yeah, but what if something happens and we do? I guess we'll tell my parents all about it, huh?" Desmond crossed one arm over the other, mirroring Corin's pose.

"You know what?" Sam sounded annoyed. "Let's just put this stuff in your parents' room and get moving. We have a big day planned for you three, and I would hate for you to miss any of it."

Desmond sighed, and he heard his two friends echo the sentiment behind him. "Fine. Where are we going first?"

"That's better. Now, as soon as we get your things put away, we'll be visiting a very nice cathedral not far from here. It has lots of cool historical stuff that I know you three will absolutely love." He was overplaying it, and the kids knew it. They knew that he thought it was probably the most boring place he could take them, a subtle revenge move to pay them back for sneaking away the day before.

What Sam didn't realize is that was exactly where the kids were planning to go in the first place.

And they had no intention of enlightening him.

"A cathedral?" Corin protested. "How boring."

"Come on, Sam," Desmond added to the fake argument. "Not that."

"Nope," Sam said. "It's already decided. I've even arranged for a tour with one of the priests. So, get your things. We're leaving immediately to get some breakfast, and then it's off to the church."

Sam ushered the three out the door and down the hallway toward the Ellerbys' room. He and Billy didn't see the mischievous smirks the three kids exchanged as they shuffled down the hall.

3

Rome

WAYNE COLLINS DIDN'T dare step out of his car. He'd seen the police presence from a block away. They were in plain clothes, but it was easy to spot a cop no matter what they wore. He had enough experience dealing with shady characters to know the difference between an ordinary citizen and someone trying to *look* like one.

There were two in front of the hotel: one on either side of the entrance. Another was posted at the side door. Wayne figured there would also be someone watching the back, so there was no point in even looking back there.

As best he could figure, the rampage through the kids' room had likely raised some alarm bells in the Ellerbys' minds. If it hadn't, then it must have been their head of security who called for the additional eyes on the street. Not that it mattered. The fact was that there was no way Wayne or his associate, Carl, was going to get into the hotel unnoticed. Not by conventional means, at least.

The three kids had gotten the better of Wayne and his henchman the night before. It resulted in an uncomfortable, wet, smelly walk back to his car followed by an even worse ride back to the hotel.

Neither man had said anything to the other, though Wayne was certain Carl was on the verge of apologizing several times.

Wayne didn't want apologies. He wanted results. Specifically, he wanted the map and whatever it was the kids had discovered in the catacombs of the temple.

How had three kids been able to get the better of him? It was a question he'd pondered nearly all night. Unable to fall asleep until the early morning hours, that question racked his brain for hours, causing him to toss and turn in his bed.

Wayne figured Carl was experiencing the same kind of insomnia, probably worse. Carl knew what happened to people who failed his boss. Wayne Collins didn't tolerate failure. Perhaps the only saving grace for Carl was that Wayne had been just as responsible.

One of the cops in front of the hotel stepped to the side to let a woman walk through the door. The doorman held it open for her until she was inside, and then he stepped back in, disappearing from view to wait for the next patron to arrive.

Out of the corner of his eye, Wayne saw his henchman staring at him for some reason.

"What?" Wayne didn't attempt to hide his irritation. He asked the question before slowly turning his head toward Carl.

"What do you think we should do, boss? I don't see how there's any way we can get in there again. They've tightened security all around the building from the looks of it."

Carl's voice sounded jittery, full of nerves.

Wayne thought Carl *should* have been nervous. Wayne was furious at the outcome of the previous night. He was tired, and on top of it all Carl was asking stupid questions and making ridiculous points.

"Thank you, Captain Obvious," Wayne said. "I can see that."

He twisted his head back around and gazed at the building. "Obviously, the Ellerbys upped security around the building. If I had to guess, there are probably more security guys on the inside, just waiting for us to make a stupid mistake and show up on their doorstep."

Carl forced a nervous swallow and nodded. "So? What's the play, boss?"

"Exactly what we've been doing since we got here. We wait."

Carl nodded and rubbed his thighs, another anxiety-filled tick he exhibited when his nerves got the better of him.

"Could you please stop doing that?" Wayne asked. It came off as more of an order in his commanding tone.

"Sorry, boss."

Carl gripped the edge of the car seat with both hands and went back to staring out the windshield at the front of the hotel.

A black SUV pulled up and stopped. The windows were darkly tinted. The wheels were a matte black color as well.

Wayne reached up and pressed the ignition button. The engine revved to life, and he placed his left hand on the wheel, the right on the gearshift.

"Undercover cops?" Carl asked.

Wayne shook his head. "No. This is something else." He furrowed his brow, trying to figure out who was in the SUV. He narrowed his eyes and continued looking out through the glass with one hand still ready to shift the car into drive if the need arose.

The driver's side door of the SUV swung open and a man in a black suit and tie with aviator sunglasses climbed out. He rushed around to the other side and flung the doors open.

"Must be someone important, eh, boss?" Carl asked.

"Maybe," Wayne said. He leaned forward slightly as if that would help him get a better view of what was happening.

The driver stood by the open rear door on the passenger side of the SUV and waited. Wayne held his breath, half expecting a foreign dignitary, celebrity, or wealthy tycoon to appear. It was none of those. And the faces that appeared in the hotel doorway as it opened were ones that excited him more than any of the other possibilities combined.

The three children from the night before walked through the door as the doorman held it open. The kids were followed by a security guard dressed in the same uniform as the SUV's driver.

"Well, well, well," Wayne said. "Look who it is."

"The kids from the other night."

Wayne rolled his eyes and sighed. "Yes, thank you for pointing that out, Carl." He said the man's name with disdain. He knew he was going to have to replace Carl at some point. While the man had been loyal, he wasn't the brightest person in the world and had the annoying habit of always stating things that were blatantly obvious to pretty much everyone else.

"And it was last night," Wayne corrected.

"Right. Sorry, boss. All runs together, you know?"

No. Wayne didn't know, but he wasn't going to perpetuate this ridiculous conversation.

He watched as the kids crossed the narrow sidewalk, looking around in both directions as the bodyguard ushered them into the SUV.

Carl slunk down into his seat, afraid someone might see and recognize him.

Wayne let out another exasperated breath and shook his head. "What are you doing?"

"I don't want them to see me, boss. You should duck down, too."

Wayne considered kicking his assistant out of the car, but he needed Carl, at least for now.

"Get up," Wayne ordered. "You look like an idiot. They can't see us from all the way over there. And even if they could, they wouldn't recognize us in this car."

"But if we can recognize them..."

"Please, stop talking," Wayne said.

Carl nodded and shimmied back to an upright position, though not as high as he was before.

They watched the kids climb into the SUV. The bodyguard behind them opened the front passenger door and got in. Then the driver slammed the door shut and hurried around to reassume his position behind the wheel. He took a quick look at the oncoming traffic, found a window, and pulled out onto the street amid the semi-chaotic Roman commute.

Wayne didn't move, nor did he turn his head to follow the SUV with his eyes as it drove by them, speeding down the road away from where they sat.

Carl twisted his head around and kept his eyes on the vehicle. "Boss? You gonna follow them or what?"

Wayne kept his gaze on the side mirror, watching the SUV until there were five, then six cars behind it along with a few scooters and motorcycles. He answered Carl's question with a quick shift of the transmission and stepped on the gas.

Carl's head rocked back and struck the headrest. He grunted at the sudden impact, a sound that made Wayne's lips crease in a wicked smile. Carl deserved that one for being so annoying.

Wayne deftly spun the steering wheel around and whipped the sedan around oncoming traffic, narrowly missing a motorcyclist who pressed his horn in a moment of fury.

Wayne didn't care. He was on the hunt now.

He guided the car into the next lane over to complete his risky U-turn and merged in with the rest of the traffic flowing toward the center of town.

"I...I can't see it, boss," Carl confessed. "We're gonna lose them." He almost sounded accusatory in the way he said it.

Wayne still saw the SUV up ahead, several cars in front of them. There was no way he was going to lose them this time. What had started as something that should have been easy had turned into a disaster. The annoying little brats in the SUV had gotten the better of them, made him look foolish. No one made Wayne Collins look foolish. No one. This was no longer just a treasure hunt. It was personal, and Wayne wanted payback.

"No," he said through his teeth. "I have them."

4

R ome

THE SUV DROVE AROUND to the side of the church, leaving the stream of traffic behind. The narrow alley was just wide enough for the SUV to fit and be able to open the doors without scratching them, but there was no way to get two cars side by side in there.

Billy stopped the vehicle, put it in park, and quickly got out to open the back door for his passengers.

Sam climbed out and walked around, giving a quick scan of the street and the sidewalk on the other side. He hadn't said a thing on the short drive to the cathedral, despite the kids asking him several times where they were going.

He stepped to the rear of the SUV and paused, watching the cars go by on the busy street until all three of his charges were out of the vehicle and standing with arms crossed on the sidewalk.

"Okay," he said with a condescending grin. "Let's go learn some stuff about this church's history and architecture. Shall we?" He motioned with his hand toward the steps leading up to the front doors of the cathedral. The kids dragged their feet and walked forward.

They didn't hear Sam order Billy to pull the SUV around to the back and then keep his eyes on the sidewalk in front of the building.

"Keep out of sight," Sam said. "Something is going on here, and I don't like it."

Billy gave a short nod and returned to the driver's seat of the SUV. He disappeared from view a few seconds later.

Desmond led the way up the steps, trudging forward like he would rather be anywhere else in the world than there. Of course, his friends knew the truth. They put on the same act as him, slinking their way up the stairs like they were miserable. Sam had no way of knowing this was exactly where they wanted to be. The only trick would be losing him for long enough to be alone with the priest, if that priest was even there at that moment.

None of the kids had any idea what a priest's schedule was like. It was reasonable to think that if the man had been there during the evening on their previous visit, maybe he wouldn't be working during the day, especially at this time of morning. It wasn't early, but it wasn't afternoon either.

At the top of the steps, they paused and waited for Sam to catch up. He rushed up to meet them and grabbed the big door handle, giving it a tug. "After you," he said, sticking out his hand again for the kids to go first.

They resumed the act and reluctantly made their way into the building. The second they were inside, the visitors felt the ancient smells of stone, wood, old fabric, and mustiness wash over them. The scents mingled with a hint of incense that wafted to the entrance from the area near the front of the sanctuary.

"Okay," Sam said, rubbing his hands and letting the door close behind him. "Where should we start?"

Desmond rolled his shoulders. "Why don't we find a priest and ask him?"

Sam stuck out his index finger at Desmond. "That's a great idea.

They can tell us all we want to know about this place." Sam's eyes darted around the atrium. He noted the sculpted stone reliefs over the three doors leading into the sanctuary, the cistern of holy water, and the candles burning on the walls. There was no one else in the room. The only people he saw were a few parishioners on their knees near the front of the sanctuary and a priest kneeling in front of a cross with an anguished figure melded to it.

"Come on," Sam said, motioning for the kids to follow.

They did as ordered as Sam walked through the open doorway on the right and into the cavernous sanctuary. He pointed at a pew to his right. "Sit here for a minute while I have a look around and try to find a priest."

The kids collectively nodded and slid into the long bench seat with their hands folded in their laps. Sam wandered off, his head turning left and right, looking for one of the monks or priests who he hoped could give them a tour.

When the bodyguard was far enough away, Desmond looked over at the other two. He wore a sense of urgency on his face, both his eyes and mouth wide. "Hey, what should we do? He's gonna be back as soon as he finds someone to show us around."

"We need to find that priest," Corin hissed.

The three craned their necks and looked to the front of the room. The priest kneeling at the foot of the cross wasn't the same one from before. They panned the room quickly and realized that the guy was nowhere to be seen. It was exactly what they'd feared.

"I don't see him," Diego said.

"Me either." Desmond pressed his lips together. He swirled his tongue against his left cheek, making it bulge slightly. It was a nervous tick he had when he was trying to come up with a solution to a tough problem. "Any ideas?"

Corin searched the room again, looking behind them and then forward again in hopes that maybe a priest or monk would appear out of thin air. Then she noticed a row of three wooden rooms to her right. They looked like external closets, each with two doors. The doors to two of the units were open, revealing narrow wooden benches inside with a cushioned prayer bench on the opposing side.

"I need to go to confession," she said.

The boys frowned.

"What?" Diego protested, a little louder than he intended. The three looked toward Sam, who was turning a corner in the aisle and making his way to an alcove on the left. "You're not Catholic." Diego lowered his voice.

"I know that," she whispered. "But there's a priest in there. Maybe it's the guy we talked to before."

"What about Sam?"

"I'll cover for you," Desmond said before she could respond. "Go. Hurry, before Sam comes back."

Corin took the piece of paper from her brother and stood up. She gave one last glance to the front where Sam had disappeared from view, then she scurried over to the confessional booth and stepped into the one that only had one open door. She hoped that meant there was a priest waiting on the other side. Corin pulled the door closed and eased into the seat.

"Um, hello?" She asked the question awkwardly, not certain how the whole confession process worked. She wondered what a priest did on the other side while waiting for a person to come confess their sins. It had to be a pretty boring part of the job.

A panel slid open, making a grinding sound of wood on wood.

"Yes, my child." The calming voice came through a mesh screen that separated her from the person on the other side. She recognized the voice immediately. It was the priest from the other night.

"Oh good, it's you," she blurted.

She saw the blurry figure on the other side turn his head toward her.

"Ah, my American friend. How is your little project going? And why are you here for confession? Not that it matters. All of God's children are welcome here."

His voice was kind, and the Italian accent only made it that much friendlier.

"Oh, sorry...um, Father. I've never done confession before."

"Nobody's perfect," he said.

She chuckled at the joke. "Actually, sir...um...Father, we found something else we were hoping you could help us with. It's another clue in Latin. Do you think you could take a second to read it?" She held up the paper to the screen window.

"This is a little strange," he said. Then a tiny drawer slid open in the wall. "But certainly. I'm always happy to help."

She folded the paper until it was the right size and then placed it in the drawer before pushing it closed. She heard the drawer open on the other side and the paper unfolding a second later.

"Ah," he said. "This is most interesting."

"What?" she asked. Her heart quickened as she was suddenly overwhelmed with concern about what the clue might have said. The last thing she wanted was to give away what they were really doing. Not that the priest would try to find the treasure for himself. Corin didn't know much about men of the cloth, but what little she did know was that they weren't the types to go after lost treasures or material pleasures. They lived simple lives, burrowed in humility and service.

She pushed aside her worries and let him finish his translation. If it said something about the treasure she and her friends sought, she wouldn't lie to him. Corin seemed to remember something about confession being confidential. She knew that meant he wouldn't tell anyone.

"This is a very interesting line," he said. "Quite the riddle."

"What is?" She asked the question a little more eagerly than she would have liked. Oh well. It was out there. Might as well keep going. "Sorry. I'm just very curious about it."

The priest cleared his throat. She could see his lips moving through the screen, though he wasn't saying anything. He was rereading the riddle.

When he spoke, his soothing voice had grown serious, cutting through the silence of the confessional booth. "It says that the second key lies beneath the monument to my enemy, the son of Neptune and scourge of the empire. Under Jupiter's gaze."

Corin frowned. What in the world did that mean? "Son of Neptune? Scourge of the empire? Jupiter's gaze?" She didn't even consider that she was saying the words out loud until they'd escaped her lips.

The priest turned and looked into the mesh screen. Then he folded the paper and put it in the little drawer, sliding it back ever so gently.

She noticed the drawer pop out and grabbed the piece of paper. She stuffed it in her pocket and started to thank the priest, but he cut her off.

"The son of Neptune. That's a very interesting clue."

"Clue?" She tried to play it off, but the second she said it Corin knew she wasn't fooling the old priest. She thought she saw a wry, knowing smile cross his lips, but through the screen it was hard to tell.

"Yes, my dear. A clue. You're searching for something. And don't worry. I'm not angry about you and your friends misleading me before."

She felt a lump catch in her throat.

"You see," he went on, "I do believe you are doing research, as you told me the other day. So, you weren't lying in that regard. I doubt very much it is a school project, though, as you would have me believe."

"I'm sorry." She muttered the words, ashamed. Guilt pumped through her veins.

"It's okay, my child. Everyone makes mistakes. In regards to your riddle, if I didn't know better, I'd say you're on a treasure hunt."

She started to protest, but there was no getting around it. This guy knew what they were up to at some level. How deep that level was, she didn't know.

"Based on what this clue suggests, I'd say the treasure you seek belonged to one of Rome's greatest and most reviled emperors. Julius Caesar was certainly a complicated man."

Corin didn't know what to say to that. She fought off the urge to dismiss his comment. "Interesting. I haven't studied him much yet. I'm only in the sixth grade, but what I know about him is that he was a great military commander and a good leader."

"Ah yes. A bit ambitious at times, which is why he was assassinated. He believed that the good of the nation no longer rested with the Senate but with him. He truly felt in his heart that only he could rule justly for Rome and that the nation would prosper far better under a monarchy than a republic."

"I never knew that." She thought for a second. "How did you know that this was about Caesar based on that riddle? It didn't say anything about him."

The priest chuckled. "My dear, if I gave you all the answers, you'd never learn a thing. And it would take the fun out of the hunt for you and your friends. Wouldn't it?"

Her lips curled into a smirk. "Yeah, I guess it would."

"The answers you seek are easily found for smart children like you three. I have no doubt you'll discover the truth soon enough. As to what treasure this might be, do not worry, I have no desire to hunt down Caesar's secret."

She was relieved to hear that even though her suspicions had already told her that would be his stance. "Thank you, Father. I appreciate your help."

"Any time, my child. I must admit this is a fascinating adventure your guild of three is embarking on. By all means, if you come across another clue, I would love to see it. I'm very interested in things of this nature, especially when it comes to the history of my city."

"Thank you," she said again. "I'd better be going."

"Yes. I'm sure your friends are concerned about how long you've been in here. They must think you quite the sinner." He chortled, and she joined in.

"I hope to speak to you again, Father."

"Me as well."

Corin stood up and pushed the door open. The warm feeling of relief that was coursing over her disappeared the second she looked up and into the sanctuary.

Sam was standing behind the two boys with a hand on their shoulders as if holding back two wild dogs.

"All done in there?" Sam asked.

"Yep," she said and stepped out of the booth. She was overwhelmed with the sense that the paper with the riddle on it was sticking out of her pocket. As naturally as she could, Corin stuffed both hands in her pockets just to make sure. The paper was down far enough to be out of sight, but that didn't keep her from feeling extremely uncomfortable under Sam's gaze.

"I didn't realize you were Catholic." The bodyguard's stare intensified.

"I'm...I'm not. I just thought it would be a good experience to try confession for a change."

Suspicion fired from his eyes like a ninja throwing stars, but she didn't back down. Corin stepped over to her friends and quickly changed the subject. "Did you find someone to show us around?"

Sam bit his lower lip and shook his head. "No, they don't really do that sort of thing here. They said we're welcome to have a look around and we can go anywhere except the private dormitory." His tone signaled he'd already let the confessional booth incident slip away. "We can stay and do that if you want, or we can take a look around somewhere else in the city. There are lots of places to check out here. I told your parents I was going to take you around all day, and I meant it."

"So...where are we going?" Desmond asked. He had to push aside the burning desire to ask Corin what she learned from the priest. Curiosity itched at every fiber of his being. He could tell Diego was suffering from the same malady.

"I don't know yet." There was frustration in Sam's voice.

Desmond knew the bodyguard wasn't a history guy. That wasn't to say he was uneducated. Sam was smart. Desmond was fully aware of that. They'd had talks in the past that had surprised Desmond, initially. Then the boy realized that Sam had a keen understanding of certain things, just not history.

Sam had a degree and a natural curiosity about things related to science. He'd been able to help Desmond solve a few problems in his little workshop more than once, usually when Desmond's parents were out looking for some buried treasure or artifact.

"Mind if I do a quick internet search for interesting places around here?" Corin asked. She did her best to mask the fact that she had a very specific set of keywords she was going to enter, all related to what she'd just learned from the priest.

"Sure," Sam said. "But let's get out of here. I don't want to be disrespectful in the church, standing around here chatting about our tourist problems." He said it with a stern tone, but there was a hint of softness in his voice, too. It was a sincerity that Corin and Diego hadn't seen in him before.

Maybe Sam wasn't so bad after all.

5

Rome

WAYNE AND CARL sat in their car across the street, catercorner from the huge cathedral. They felt safe behind their tinted windows, keeping a close eye on the church and its entrance.

"What do you think they're doing in there?" Carl asked, nearly sitting in Wayne's lap as he leaned across the center console to get a better view. His arm was brushing against Wayne's for what must have been the tenth time.

Wayne jerked away and pushed Carl back with his elbow. "Do you mind? Have you ever heard of personal space?"

"Sorry, boss."

"Stop saying you're sorry and just quit touching me. It's weird."

"Sorry...I mean, yes, boss."

Wayne rolled his eyes and leaned nearer to the window, fully expecting his assistant to get too close again. He didn't answer Carl's question because he didn't have an answer. Wayne was wondering the exact same thing. What were the kids doing in there?

Was the church somehow part of the equation? Was there a secret hidden away somewhere inside, perhaps in a series of complex catacombs under the foundation? He doubted the latter. Most the catacombs were places that had been built long after the fall of the Roman Empire. They were ancient in terms of modern times, but as far as the grand scope of history they weren't as old as other places.

He sensed Carl was going to ask the question again and cut him off by speaking first. "I wonder if that bodyguard knows what they're up to."

"You think he does?"

"I'm not sure. Based on previous events, I'd say they're doing their best to keep him out of the loop. The fewer adults who know, the better."

"Really? Sounds like a tough thing for three little kids to do."

"These aren't ordinary kids," Wayne said. "They got the better of us, didn't they?"

Carl nodded, ashamed.

"Yes, these children are special, that's for certain. And they don't seem to be afraid of anything. Could you imagine going into that dark, grimy temple we were in yesterday at their age? I couldn't."

"Not me, boss. I was scared of the dark when I was a kid," Carl confessed.

Wayne snorted. "You're scared of the dark now, Carl." He spat the name.

"That's not true."

"Sure it isn't." Wayne decided to let the ribbing end and focused his attention back on the door to the church. "Still, these are no ordinary children. They were smart enough to sneak out of that hotel and out of the museum. They were clever enough to slip away from their overpaid babysitters. And like I said, they bested us once. That won't happen again."

Carl thought for a moment. "You think they're playing the two bodyguards?"

Wayne's head bobbed slowly. "I do. That, or they told them what they're up to. Doubtful. The Ellerbys would never allow it. We play a dangerous game. The Ellerbys do, too, and they know that all too well."

"So...they're playing the bodyguards."

"We'll find out soon enough. We just have to wait until those two suits slip up. When they do, we'll be ready to pounce."

Carl gave an absent nod in agreement. The car fell silent for a minute or two before he spoke again. "Where did the other guy go?"

Wayne rolled his eyes again. What was he, a mind reader, a guy with psychic locating powers? "I'm sure I haven't the foggiest, Carl. Can you just sit there for five minutes without saying anything? Watch the front door. That's all you have to do, watch the front door."

"Yes, boss. Sorry," he started to apologize again and realized he was doing it. "I mean, right."

Wayne kept his eyes locked on the entrance for what seemed like forever. To his credit, Carl didn't say another word. Wayne knew it had to be difficult for his henchman. The guy couldn't shut up to save his life unless that's what he thought he was doing: saving his life.

Several minutes passed, and with each one Wayne grew more and more concerned.

He twisted his wrist and glanced at his expensive watch. A frown wrinkled his face and forehead. "I don't get it," he said at last.

Carl said nothing for fear of being reprimanded again.

"They've been in there too long."

"Maybe they're taking a tour."

That was the first intelligent thing Carl had said all day, maybe in the last month.

"Possibly," Wayne said, though he was unwilling to give Carl any credit. "But why would they do that if they'd just found a key piece to this whole puzzle?"

"They're kids, boss. Maybe they didn't have a choice."

"Or maybe they really haven't told the bodyguards yet."

Carl was two for two with his last couple of comments. Both made a ton of sense. That still didn't answer where the second bodyguard took the SUV, or where he was. They hadn't seen him return. More than a few times, Wayne considered getting out of the sedan and going into the church. He knew that was a foolish idea. The kids would recognize him and Carl immediately. Then the jig would be up. No, he had to sit here in his car and wait it out until the children reappeared.

"Um, boss?" Carl interrupted his thoughts.

Wayne turned and faced his assistant with a scowl. "What now?"

Carl pointed at the road in front of them. The SUV they'd been following had merged over to the right lane and kept moving down the street.

"Wasn't that the same vehicle they came in?"

Wayne winced in anger. He pushed the ignition button and shifted the car into drive. A quick glance in the mirror, and they were off, speeding out of the parking spot with tires squealing.

Wayne cut off a guy on a scooter with his sudden move. The rider swerved, narrowly missing the sedan by mere inches. He yelled a bunch of things in Italian and made several hand gestures. Wayne didn't care. He didn't speak Italian, and even if he did, why should he bother worrying about some random dude on a scooter? They had a priceless treasure to find.

He glanced in the rearview mirror one last time as he left the rider in his dust. Then Wayne put all his attention on the fleeting glimpses of his target a dozen or so cars ahead of them. He knew how to tail someone. It was something he'd picked up on long ago. Stay just close enough to keep fragments of the target vehicle in sight, but not so close that they notice you.

Types like the Ellerbys' bodyguards were trained to look for people following them, but they weren't highly trained. They would give a cursory look back now and then. While Wayne's car was certainly a luxury sedan, it didn't stand out so much that the bodyguards would pay it much attention. Besides, they were so far back it would just blend right in with all the other traffic.

The SUV veered right and entered another street, and for a moment the vehicle was in full view. They didn't seem to be in any hurry, which was good. That meant Wayne was doing exactly what he should. They weren't spooked by anything. If they had been, the SUV would be speeding away by now.

He reached the next intersection and made the turn, falling in line behind a produce delivery truck and several other cars ahead of it. Even better. A big truck like that would keep them out of sight. Sure, it made seeing the Ellerby SUV tougher, but that was fine. Now and then, Wayne would twist the steering wheel to get a quick glimpse of the target to make sure it was still on the same street and then steer back to the right to stay out of view.

"Where you think they're going now, boss?" Carl asked in a sheepish voice, almost like he was frightened.

"No idea, but stay on your toes. The second those bodyguards are out of sight, or when we get one of them alone, we pounce."

"You think that's a good call? I mean...I'm not questioning your decisions, boss. Just saying we might have one guy outnumbered, but aren't they highly trained?"

Wayne snickered. "They're rent-a-cops, Carl. Nothing more. These guys are one step away from riding around on one of those ridiculous two-wheeled things at the mall."

"Yeah...I guess you're right."

"I am. So be ready. When the time comes, we take out the guard, and then we take whatever those little brats took from us at the temple."

6

R ome

BILLY GUIDED the car down the street away from the big cathedral. Sam held on to the handle over the passenger side door out of habit. Something he always did when he was riding with someone else. It wasn't that Billy was a bad driver, though the traffic in Rome certainly caused him to make a few sudden moves that he normally wouldn't back in the United States.

"So, where is this place again?" Sam asked, glancing over his shoulder into the backseat.

Corin sighed. "Campo Marzio? You guys have to know what that is. It's a pretty famous place."

"Nope," Sam shook his head once. "Never heard of it."

"Me either," Billy said. It was the first time he'd spoken out loud in hours. The guy almost never seemed to talk. The kids collectively wondered if that was a requirement when on duty, or he was not a chatty person.

The truth was that Corin hadn't heard of it, either. The only reason she now knew was because of the search she'd done when they climbed back into the SUV. She'd made quick work of her internet search, first looking for the son of Neptune. That hadn't given a ton of help at first, not until she entered a few more details into the search bar.

Typing in the phrase "enemy of Caesar" along with the Neptune thing had produced one very significant result.

Pompey.

He was known to most as Pompey the Great. One of the great leaders of the late Republican Era of Rome, Pompey had commanded a large segment of the army. It was such a significant portion of the military that he and Julius Caesar went toe to toe in a violent civil war. Pompey was, according to the information she discovered, an incredibly talented military leader and was credited with many great victories.

Corin thought she'd heard of him before, but only in passing. Now, they were headed to Campo Marzio, the place that was the former home of Pompey's Theater.

The clue the priest had translated said that the next key would be located at the memorial of Caesar's scourge, or enemy. Son of Neptune only helped solidify that. She'd searched for Pompey's burial place since that made the most sense when referring to the word "memorial" in the clue. However, no results came up. The only thing she could find that might be a lasting tribute to the man was the enormous theater he built.

The last part of the clue still eluded her. She wasn't sure what it meant by Jupiter's gaze. Even though Corin was sitting next to both of the boys, she knew she couldn't ask them anything. Not yet. Sam was watching them like an owl eyeing a field mouse at dusk. If she mentioned anything about the clue or the riddles within, he'd know they were up to something. For the moment, she was on her own.

Corin frowned as she stared at the phone screen. She was staring at an image known as Campo Marzio.

"What is that?" Desmond asked.

"The place we're going," she answered. "Campo Marzio."

Diego frowned, craning his neck so he could get a better view. "It looks like nothing but a crowded bunch of buildings."

Corin agreed with a nod. "Yeah. I guess as the city developed over the centuries, they must have knocked down the majority of the theater." She closed her phone and slid it back in her pocket. "It has to be there, though."

"Why's that?" Sam pried from the front seat. "Why does it have to be there?"

Corin realized she'd inadvertently given away too much information with her intense focus on the location of the theater.

"Oh...because..." The kids froze.

"Because it's a historically significant place," Diego finished her explanation. "You can't just knock down one of the most famous structures in history because you need property. Right?"

Sam raised an eyebrow and turned back around to face forward. He didn't say anything, which the kids didn't know how to take. He could have remained silent because he didn't believe the explanation. Or it could have been that he simply didn't care. Either way, the three would need to be more careful.

Billy kept driving, winding his way through the mayhem that was Rome's traffic. The drive took them nearly twenty minutes of stop-and-go traffic until they reached the place on the SUV's navigation screen that was identified as Campo Marzio.

He pulled off to the side of the street, finding a tight parking spot vacated just moments before by one of the zillions of scooters that seemed to occupy the city. He pulled in nose first, knowing that if he tried the standard way of parallel parking, someone behind him would zip in there before he could.

It took several turns and adjustments, but eventually Billy got the vehicle situated, albeit only a foot or so between the cars in front and back.

"So," Sam asked, turning around again to face the kids, "what are we here to see?"

Corin and the others were looking out the windows. They were completely surrounded by residential buildings, shops, and cafés. While the structures were far from new, most probably dating back several hundred years, there was nothing that looked like it came from ancient Rome.

"I don't understand," she said. "It should be here."

She dragged the phone out of her pocket again and switched on the screen. Then she looked at multiple images, trying to locate any remains of the Theater of Pompey. The more she looked, the more disheartened she became. A rising tide of disappointment swelled in her chest.

"Is it okay if we get out and look around?" Corin asked.

Sam sighed. "Sure." He turned to Billy. "Mind staying here with the car?"

"Nope," Billy answered with one word.

"Okay, then. Come on."

Sam got out of the car, followed by the three friends. They huddled around him as he waited for them to make a decision.

"You know, there are lots of other places you can visit in this city," he said. "There's literally history everywhere. What's so special about this place?"

They shook their heads at the same time, looking up at him while trying to do their best to appear innocent. It didn't work.

"Okay," Sam said. He turned his head and looked across the street at some random spot, collecting his thoughts. Then he turned back to the kids. He had made sure Billy was out of sight, wondering if the kids were more comfortable with him now. "Something is going on here, and I want to know what it is. Does this have to do with what happened to your room yesterday?"

The three bit their lips. Diego gazed off into the distance somewhere, thinking that any eye contact would betray the truth. Desmond's eyes rolled from left to right, settling on a coffee shop where several people were standing in line inside, waiting to place their order.

They were all terrible at hiding anything.

Sam crossed his arms and replaced the curious expression on

his face with a stern one. "Listen, I know about the room incident. And I know that you three were up to something last night. I didn't tell your parents, partly because I would get in as much trouble as you if they found out you went missing in a foreign city for a few hours. But if you three don't start talking about whatever it is you're up to, I'm going to have to fall on the sword and tell them every-thing, including that I believe you were sneaking around in the museum."

One by one, the kids exchanged glances with each other, every one of them silently questioning whether or not they should tell Sam.

Sam could see they were still mulling over the choice of keeping whatever secret they possessed or filling him in on the details. He decided to try a different tack.

"Look, guys. If you're in some kind of trouble, I can help. If you did something you weren't supposed to, I might be able to help with that, too. I don't want this trip to be a pain for any of us, but right now, with you keeping whatever secret you're keeping, it's gonna be a long couple of weeks. For all of us. I don't want to keep going on being mean like this. Let me help you."

Part of what he said appealed to the three kids. Every single one of them considered what Sam was saying, especially the part about him helping if they were in some kind of trouble. The two men who'd tried to take the map and the stone from them were clearly up to no good. If they returned, that *would* be big trouble. No doubt the two guys were angry at having been bested by three middle-schoolers. Adults hated that sort of thing.

Desmond knew that from playing online video games against older people. They would always get furious when he'd beat them and then learn he was only in sixth grade.

If those guys returned, somehow, or found out where Desmond and his friends were or what they were up to, their next encounter might not end so well. Even last time one of them had pulled a gun. There was no telling what the two men might do if they crossed paths again.

He searched his friends' faces for an answer. Desmond could tell they were thinking the same thing.

Diego and Corin nodded their approval.

When Desmond spoke, the words came out like water from a fire hose.

"We're looking for the lost treasure of Julius Caesar, and there were two men who tried to take the clues from us, but we somehow got away from them and now we don't know where they are or what we should do next because, apparently, the clue we found was leading to a place that no longer exists." He nearly ran out of breath and had to take a long, deep inhale to recover.

Sam's eyebrows stitched together, though his stoic expression remained the same. "What?"

The other two kids were just as shocked as the bodyguard. They were willing to share some information with Sam, sure, but Desmond had just spilled the entire can of beans.

Before Corin or Diego could explain or maybe correct their friend, Sam shook his head and cut them off.

"Fine. I can see you aren't going to be honest with me. I was hoping we could come to some kind of understanding. Looks like you're going to make me do this the hard way."

The kids frowned. The realization came only a moment later.

"You...don't believe him?" Diego asked.

Corin wanted to elbow her brother, but she restrained herself.

Sam let out a booming laugh. "Seriously? Lost treasure of Julius Caesar? Two men trying to take the clues from you? Come on. Tell me the truth, guys. This is your last chance."

"I'm serious," Desmond insisted. "That's really what happened!"

Sam sighed. He was done playing games and being toyed with. "Fine. Where did you find this clue?" The last word came accompanied with a mocking pair of air quotes.

Desmond turned to Corin and motioned to her with his hand. He gave an encouraging nod to Diego.

"Maybe...we should get back in the car first and go somewhere a little less crowded," Corin suggested.

Sam clenched his jaw, irritation building on his face. He looked around and spotted a café with empty seats and tables on the sidewalk. Through the window, he could see the café was mostly vacant.

"How about we go in there. It looks quiet."

The kids followed his gaze, looked at each other, and then nodded.

"Fine," Corin said.

She scanned the street and the sidewalk one last time to make sure they weren't being followed. While he didn't say anything about it right away, Sam noticed. His eyes narrowed in suspicion.

"Okay. We'll go talk in there, but no more lies. I want to know what is going on, and I want to know the truth."

The kids led the way to the café with their bodyguard in tow. When they reached the door, Sam stepped in front of them and opened it.

Once Diego, the last one to enter, was inside, he took a quick glance around. If Corin was concerned enough to check for trouble, maybe they weren't lying after all.

7

Rome

CORIN MADE her way over to a table in the back corner of the café and found a seat facing the front. Diego sat next to her with Desmond sitting with his back to the door.

"What do you guys want?" Sam asked. "I'm buying."

"Nothing for me, thanks," Diego said.

Sam arched an eyebrow. "You know, this is a business. You need to have something. I don't think they'd appreciated us coming in here and sitting around without buying a drink or a pastry."

"Fine," Diego sighed. "I'll have a hot chocolate." Then he spied the display of pastries and suddenly became very interested in what the shop had to offer. "And a biscotti."

Sam grinned. "What about you two?"

"Same," Corin said.

"I'll have that, too." Desmond gave a nod.

"All right then. Three hot chocolates and three biscotti." He motioned to Corin with his index finger. "And you're in my seat. When I come back, you need to be next to him." He pointed at Desmond.

"What?" She looked confused. "Why?"

Sam turned his head and stared out the window for a moment. "Because whatever has you spooked doesn't need to catch me from behind. I always keep the windows and doors facing me. Smart of you to do that, by the way. Don't think I didn't notice. And don't think I didn't see your paranoid reconnaissance out on the sidewalk. Trust me, if there really is someone following you, you want me to see them first."

"Fine," she relented. Corin got up and slid into the chair next to Desmond. Corin was finally beginning to trust Sam a little more now.

"Good. I'll be right back."

Sam made his way over to the counter where a young Italian woman with smooth black hair secured in a ponytail was standing behind the register. He chatted politely with her for a minute before pointing at the menu and then at some of the pastries in the display. She continued smiling at him, which caused the kids to wonder if Sam was hitting on her or just being a handsome tourist.

"What's his deal?" Corin asked, staring at the interaction over her shoulder.

"What do you mean?" Desmond's eyebrows pinched together.

"You know. He's mean, then nice, then mean again. Right now he's being sweet to that girl behind the counter. So, what's his deal?"

"Oh, I got ya. Yeah, he's a bodyguard. Used to be in private security with someone else, then my parents hired him. I don't know what he did before that, but I know he had some pretty good training. Probably in the army or something. Anyway, he tries to be strict all the time. I think because it's safer that way. He's a nice person, though, once you get to know him."

"I imagine people like that probably have to keep up certain appearances to do their job," Diego offered.

"I guess." Desmond shrugged. "It's not just an appearance with Sam. He really is a tough guy. It comes across as mean to us, but he's just trying to keep us safe. I know he means well."

"Now I feel bad for lying to him before."

"We didn't lie."

"We weren't exactly honest, either."

"I guess you're right," Desmond said with a dejected nod. "Honesty really is the best policy."

"Yeah. From now on, we need to do better with that."

Sam collected a tray of the pastries and drinks and returned to the table with a thin smile on his face.

"Okay, here you go." He slid the tray onto the table and sat next to Diego, facing the window. "Dig in."

Each of the kids took a steaming cup of rich hot chocolate and a biscotti. Sam grabbed a coffee and a piece of coffee cake. He took a bite and then set the dessert back on a napkin, sipped a swig of coffee, and then folded his fingers.

"Now," he said, "tell me what you three are up to. And why the secrecy?"

Corin swallowed hard and gave a nod to her brother. She reached in her pocket and produced the piece of paper, sliding it across the table to the bodyguard.

"This is what we found yesterday," Diego said. "Well, we wrote down the clue on the thing we found."

Sam had been expecting some kind of hoax, maybe a kids' toy or something, but the words on this piece of paper were written in Latin. As far as he knew, they didn't speak Latin.

He leaned forward and frowned, picking up the paper to examine it more closely. "What is that?" Genuine curiosity filled his voice.

"It's a clue to a key," Corin explained. "Desmond wasn't lying. We found a map in the ship my parents have in the museum. The map led us to a piece of stone in an ancient temple. We went there last night and found it."

"A key?" Sam's eyes shifted up from the stone and searched her face for a lie. He'd been in the security business for several years, but before that he'd worked for the government. Sam had spent enough time with liars to know one when he saw one. Kids, he assumed, were worse at it than adults. That assumption was being tested at the moment by a sixth-grade girl.

Corin answered with a nod.

He couldn't find a single shred of evidence in her eyes that suggested she was lying.

Sam returned his gaze to the piece of paper. A flat expression on his face turned sour as he tried to wrap his head around everything.

"Are you telling me that you guys broke into the secure vault area of the museum, climbed around on that ship your parents found, and then tampered with it? Then on top of that, you went running around a foreign city, searching for what you think is a lost treasure?"

He looked up, and the kids nodded.

"Where is this stone now?"

"Back at the hotel, along with the map." Desmond hoped Sam wasn't angry. More than that, he prayed the bodyguard wouldn't tell his parents. "Where you told us to put it."

Sam's eyes blinked rapidly. He processed everything and then stood up, leaving the note on the table's surface. "I'll be right back. Don't move." The stern, almost parental tone the kids had gotten used to had returned.

Sam walked back over to the café counter and put on his best fake smile. He chatted with the woman behind the register for nearly five minutes, bobbing his head, using his hands to emphasize points, and then thanking her when the conversation was over.

"What was that about?" Corin asked as Sam strode across the floor.

The boys rolled their shoulders.

Sam slid back into his seat and put his elbows on the table, interlocking his fingers. "She said that Pompey's Theater has been gone for a long time. There's barely anything left of it under the modern city. Your clue is a dead end."

He took a sip of coffee and narrowed his eyes against the sunlight coming through the windows.

The kids exchanged searching glances with each other.

"Wait," Desmond said. "That's it? You're not gonna tell Mom and Dad?"

Sam set his coffee down and looked into the brown liquid for a second. When he looked up, there was a glint of mischief in his eyes.

"Look, I like my job. I like your parents. They've been good to me and Billy. The last thing I want to do is upset them. You guys could have been hurt, though, and I don't know who these men are you're talking about, but if they're the ones who ransacked your room I'd say they're dangerous. I don't know if what you said about this...temple and whatever you claim you found there is true, but if it is I think it's best to leave it alone."

Dejected expressions washed over the faces of all three kids. Corin looked down at the table. Diego slumped and rested his chin on his palm. Desmond chewed on his lower lip.

"Are you the one who had all those cops around the hotel earlier this morning?" Desmond asked the question out of the blue.

Sam snorted. "No. Apparently, some foreign dignitary was there. Although, if what you're telling me about those two men is real, I'd say it wouldn't be a bad idea to up the security detail." He leaned to the left and looked out beyond a couple sitting in the middle of the room, laughing and drinking espressos. "Now you have me wondering if they're still around." There was concern in his voice.

He turned his gaze to Corin. "Earlier, when we left, you were looking around just before you got in the SUV. You think they were there, don't you?"

"I didn't see anything unusual," Corin said quickly. "But I was a little worried."

Sam gave a nod. "Well, we're going to drop this." He tapped his finger on the paper. "Like I said, the theater no longer exists. So, if you three really did find a...what did you call it?"

"A key," Diego answered.

"Right. A key. If you did find something like that, it's a dead end. There's nothing for you here. So, I hope you enjoyed your little adventure, but it's time to go back to being regular tourists. Okay?"

He took another sip of his coffee as the kids sat and quietly contemplated their next move. The disappointment on their faces was palpable. Sam didn't care. His job was to keep them safe, not entertained, and certainly not to encourage them to go traipsing around Rome in search of ancient treasures while trying to evade who knew what kind of people.

Corin pulled out her phone and opened the search app again. She started reading through some of the results and then found one that looked interesting. She tapped it and scanned the page, reading the sentences rapidly. There was a small picture of a computer rendering. It resembled what historians believed the Pompey Theater to look like.

"What are you doing?" Diego asked as he shoved the last piece of biscotti into his mouth.

She held up a finger, telling him to wait a minute.

Sam acted disinterested but glanced sideways at her, only the slightest bit curious. He figured she was looking for something else for them to do that day.

"Find anything interesting?" He asked the question and then followed it with a chuckle.

"Actually, yes."

"Good. Glad to see you're ready to move on from this wild goose...whatever you were doing."

"But it's a little north of here in a town called Sorano. You and Billy up for a little drive through Tuscany?"

Sam narrowed his eyes, suspicious. "Where are you wanting to go?"

"There's a museum there. It's inside a fortress. I thought maybe we could check it out. It's one of the only fortresses in all of Italy that never fell to an enemy."

Sam sighed. "There are plenty of museums and historical places for you guys to check out here." He shook his head and took another swig of coffee. "Pick one of those. I doubt your parents want us taking you out of the city."

Desmond played along with Corin. He craned his neck to the side and raised his palms. "I don't know. I always thought parents wanted kids to get outside more, out in nature. Being stuck in the city kind of goes against that, doesn't it? Maybe they would be happy to hear you're taking us out into the country. It's much safer out there."

Sam's curiosity escalated. He was also impressed at the argumentative abilities of these kids. Some adults viewed children as simpleminded. These kids were clearly not that. They were advanced thinkers. Perhaps adults were wrong about children. Maybe they weren't as simple as he himself once thought.

"No, Corin," Sam said. "I want to know the real reason you're interested in this place."

He saw right through her ploy.

"Fine," she relented. "The Orsini family bought the land where the theater used to be. I was thinking that...if they owned the place when it was torn down, maybe they salvaged some things from there before the newer construction went up. It's worth a shot. Maybe we find this second key there; maybe we don't. If you take us there and we don't find anything, we'll come back to Rome and forget all this ever happened. And we won't bring it up again."

He lowered his eyebrows. "You see, you don't get to negotiate with me. I'm the adult. I make the decisions."

She shrugged and looked to the side, giving a nonchalant expression. "That's fine. We'll just tell Desmond's parents everything and see how that goes. I'm sure we'll be grounded when we get back to America, but it's worth it to find out whether or not I'm right about this."

Desmond and Diego widened their eyes in surprise.

Sam just sat there for a moment in stunned silence. She was leveraging him, and he didn't like it. Where did this girl learn how to do that?

He thought hard for a couple of minutes before he responded. When he did, his angry, muted tone had returned. "I don't like your attitude, young lady. What you're doing is blackmailing me. That's not cool. And you're threatening me. I don't take kindly to threats."

"There's no harm in it, Sam. You want to take us around to see the sights? Then do it. All I'm asking is to let us check out this museum. If there's nothing of interest, we drop the case."

"So, it's a case now? What are you, some kind of historical investigators now?"

"No," Corin said. She recalled the words of the priest when they'd spoken earlier that morning. "We're the Adventure Guild."

8

Rome

WAYNE AND CARL watched the kids and their bodyguard through the windows of the café. The driver of the SUV was still sitting behind the wheel, looking at his phone.

"What are they doing?" Carl asked.

"They're drinking coffee and eating some pastries," Wayne answered. He did little to disguise the annoyance in his voice.

"Coffee?" Carl looked surprised. "Those kids are drinking coffee? I don't remember liking coffee at that age. And who lets their kids drink coffee? Won't that make them too hyper or something?"

"Fine, Carl. Maybe they're drinking hot cocoa or something. Do you really think it matters what's in their cups? They're sipping something and eating something. Okay?" His voice nearly roared in the quiet confines of the sedan.

"You don't have to get testy. I just thought it was weird."

Wayne wished he'd gotten rid of Carl and brought in someone

less irritating. It was too late for that now. Maybe this would be the last job for Carl.

Wayne turned back and looked through his window and into the café. The girl produced something from her pocket and put it on the table for the bodyguard, but from that distance Wayne couldn't tell what it was. It looked like a piece of paper. He had no clue what could be on it.

After a little more discussion, the bodyguard stood up again and walked over to the counter. He talked with the girl behind the register for a few minutes. If Wayne didn't know better, he'd have thought the bodyguard was hitting on the barista. He doubted that was the case. The Ellerbys' head of security wouldn't be so foolish, especially with the three children right next to him.

Frustration swelled in Wayne's gut and rose into his chest. Would these guys never leave the kids alone? Not even for five seconds?

The bodyguard finished his conversation with the barista and returned to the table. For a moment, Wayne thought the girl's brother saw them, but the boy engaged with the group's conversation so Wayne shrugged off the paranoia.

There was no way the kid noticed them. The windows were too darkly tinted for the kid to see through, especially from another window and from that distance.

Sensing his assistant was about to ask another question, Wayne cut him off. "The bodyguard went back to the table and is talking with the kids again."

"I see that."

Of course he did.

"I wish we knew what they were saying," Carl said.

"Wouldn't that be helpful?" Wayne let the words spew with venom.

"Sure would, boss."

Wayne rolled his eyes and focused on the group inside the café. A few minutes went by before they stood up and started for the door. Wayne started the engine, ready to resume following the SUV.

"I guess we keep after them," he said. "I wonder what in the world they're up to."

"What if they give up, boss?"

Wayne hadn't even considered that. They'd come all the way to this part of town to get coffee and desserts? Why? There were plenty of places closer to their hotel, most just as good or better than the little café they were now leaving. What was so special about this place?

"What's the name of this part of town, Carl?" He asked the question rapidly, with a sudden sense of urgency.

"I don't know, boss. One second." He pulled out his phone and looked at the map. A blue dot blinked on the screen next to the words Campo Marzio. He said the name of the location, but it didn't ring a bell to Wayne.

"What is so important that they came all the way over here?"

"Maybe they were trying to throw us off," Carl offered. "You know, throw us off the trail, make us wonder what they're up to when, really, they're not up to anything."

"That might be the smartest thing you've said so far, Carl."

"Thanks, boss."

The right-hand man clearly didn't catch the scathing tone of the fake compliment.

"It makes sense, though," Wayne continued. "There's no way their babysitter is going to take them around the city, looking for a lost treasure. And if they said anything about what happened last night, those guards will be extra careful. No, I think the trail may have just gone cold."

Wayne sighed. He'd wanted this more than anything since the moment he realized the kids had found a treasure map inside the ancient Roman vessel. He'd never desired something more in his life, now that he thought about it. Finding that treasure would not only add to his already significant fortune, but it would finally give him the fame and recognition he'd always wanted.

Now it seemed the trail had gone cold. They could always go back to the original plan, taking some of the relics from the Ellerbys' collection and ruining their huge exhibit.

To say it was disappointing would be a huge understatement. Now, going back to the original plan would be a huge letdown. Not only that, but things had changed. The bodyguards would likely have made adjustments due to the glitch in the security system from before. No, things would be much more difficult now. Wayne felt like giving up.

Carl was looking at his phone as Wayne watched the kids and their bodyguard exit the café, walk down the sidewalk, and get into the vehicle.

"Boss?" Carl was looking over at Wayne.

Wayne was deep in thought when Carl snapped him out of it. "This place isn't insignificant."

"What do you mean?" Wayne saw the kids disappear into the SUV as the bodyguards shut the doors and climbed in the front.

He turned and found Carl staring at him with his phone tilted his way.

"What is that?" Wayne asked, narrowing his eyes to focus better on whatever it was his second-in-command was trying to show him.

"This used to be the location of Pompey's Theater."

Wayne blinked in disbelief. "How do you know about Pompey?"

Carl frowned. "I study history."

Wayne kept his bluff-calling glare firm.

"Okay, I don't really know who he is...or was. But he was a famous Roman, right? I mean, if they built a theater in tribute to him."

Wayne whipped his head around in time to see the SUV pull out of its parking space and drive off. He shifted the sedan into gear and waited a second until an opening appeared in the line of cars coming his way. He jerked the wheel and spun the vehicle around, following the SUV with the three kids inside.

"What's going on?" Carl asked. There was a new sense of concern in his voice.

"Pompey," Wayne said, "was one of the greatest military commanders of his time. He was initially an ally of Julius Caesar."

"Okay..." Carl clearly didn't understand why he needed a history lesson at that particular moment.

"They worked together for a time, but the two men had enormous egos. Both wanted total control of the republic. As military men, they both believed they could rule and expand the empire in ways only they understood. They also considered the Senate to be obsolete. They figured the best, most efficient way to run an empire was with one absolute ruler who controlled everything, made all the critical decisions. The republic system slowed things down. Pompey, however, had the backing of the Senate, and so he played along, knowing that if he became Rome's savior, he could assume more and more power."

"So...why are we leaving that area then if that's where Pompey's Theater was?"

"Well, I'm glad you asked." He turned the wheel to the right in the direction he'd seen the SUV go a few seconds before.

"Pompey and Caesar became bitter rivals. They were embroiled in a civil war that ravaged the republic and divided it in half. Men who'd once served together in the army were pitted against one another in a bloody conflict."

"Who won?"

Wayne rolled his eyes for what seemed like the millionth time. "Caesar, Carl. Caesar won."

"Oh." Carl's face creased with a stupid smile. "That's good."

"Anyway, Pompey was disgraced and in trouble after he blew a huge chance to win the civil war. He had greater numbers than Caesar, but Caesar was a better tactician. Pompey's army was routed, and the leader fled to Egypt, where he was assassinated by King Ptolemy. Pompey had gone from being one of the most powerful men in the world to a political outcast and a failure by the time he died."

"That sounds awful."

"Yeah, sure," Wayne said as callously as he could. "Anyway, Caesar probably had a big hand in the destruction of anything remotely related to Pompey. He probably ordered that the place be torn down, but I don't really recall the rest of the story after that."

Carl listened patiently and waited for a minute before he spoke up again. They were driving rapidly through the city, and it appeared, based on the turns and the direction the SUV was taking, they were going north.

"So...what are we doing now, boss?"

"We're taking a gamble," Wayne said.

"A gamble?"

"That's right. See, I think those kids are onto something. Maybe their handlers know about it. Maybe they don't. But they were in that part of town for a reason. If they happened to think that the old Pompey Theater had something to do with Caesar's treasure, then I'm willing to bet they figured out another clue."

"So, that's your gamble?"

Wayne nodded. "Absolutely."

"I don't mean to be rude, boss, but that sounds like a bit of a stretch to me. You really think these kids are so persistent? Most kids their age give up when the going gets tough."

Wayne knew his assistant was right. Kids, at least the ones he knew of, usually retreated in the face of adversity. They preferred the path of least resistance. Okay, that was true of most adults, too. These kids, though, there was something about them. They didn't seem like the types to give up easily. Thus the situation Wayne and Carl currently found themselves in.

"You're right, Carl. Most kids would have given up long ago. Then again, how many kids their age do you see with such a strong interest in history? Did you care about history or finding artifacts when you were their age? I know I didn't. I was too busy playing cricket."

"I was playing football," Carl said, his voice reflecting a hint of dejection.

"Exactly."

The SUV made a quick left turn at the next intersection and continued moving north, away from downtown.

"Maybe I'm wrong," Wayne confessed. "But my money is on them finding another clue. And if they did, this time we'll be there to snatch whatever they find right out of their hands."

"What about the bodyguards?"

"Leave them to me."

9

S orano

THE DRIVE to Sorano took a little over two hours. Not too bad, except that most of the journey was made in silence. That made things considerably more boring.

The kids and Sam had agreed on the walk back to the SUV that they would let Billy in on what was happening. They trusted Sam a lot more than they had when they arrived. He had gone from the mean, stern babysitter to the stern but slightly nicer bodyguard. It was a nice change.

And the views on this drive were spectacular. The rolling Italian countryside looked like a moving postcard out the windows of the SUV. The kids stared out at vineyards, mountains, hills, villas, castles, and little towns they passed along the way.

If they thought all that stuff was cool, everyone in the car, including the two adults, were blown away when they arrived at the village of Sorano. The beige stonework seemed to have been used on every building, including the cathedral. The citizenry's dwellings were stacked close together and towered over a river at the base of a cliff. A few bell towers with terracotta roofing stood out above everything else.

The green hills surrounding the little medieval town framed the tan outcropping of buildings like a painting, offering a stunning contrast between ancient human building techniques and nature's lush display.

"This place is so old," Diego blurted.

Billy steered the car up the last quarter mile of winding road until he came to a place where it appeared tourists parked their cars. Sorano, it seemed, was a mostly pedestrian village with tightly packed alleys, corridors, and thoroughfares.

After the SUV's engine was off, the kids climbed out of the car and onto the cobblestone street. They gazed toward the town and a long row of steps leading up to the village center.

Visitors were busy taking pictures, taking in the vistas, and looking at maps to find places of interest.

"I like it," Desmond said out of the blue. He directed his comment at Corin.

"Like what?" she asked, a quizzical look on her face.

"The Adventure Guild. I meant to tell you before, but they weren't in a good mood so I thought keeping quiet was the right call." He jerked his thumb at the two bodyguards who were getting out of the car and making sure they had everything they needed, which wasn't much.

Corin grinned. "Yeah, it just came to me. I think it was something the priest said that gave me the idea."

"I like it, too," Diego said with a nod.

"Okay, young 'uns. Where to? We've already wasted a couple hours driving up here." Sam glanced down at his watch. "I'd say you can have two hours here, and then we need to head back. Your parents want you at the hotel by dinner, and I doubt they'd like it if I told them where we were."

Sam seemed almost afraid of the Ellerbys, a point that Desmond found interesting since his parents came off as some of the least threatening people he knew. Although he was biased.

"We shouldn't need more than that," Corin said. "Come on. Let's find the castle."

"Castle?" Sam shook his head. "If you wanted to see a castle, we passed like ten of them on the way here."

"Not this one."

She started off toward some steps. Sam glanced at Billy. "Wanna watch the car?"

Billy shrugged. "Nah. I'll tag along."

"Suit yourself. It should be fine here. I didn't notice anyone following us."

The kids were already on the steps, making their way up toward the village's main street.

"You don't actually believe what they were saying, do you? About the two guys and all that?" Billy arched an eyebrow in suspicion.

Sam turned his head and looked back over his shoulder. He panned the area behind them for a moment and then faced Billy. "No. I don't think there are two men after them. But there's no harm in exercising a little extra caution. Just keep your eyes peeled."

"So, you think there *are* a couple of men after them."

Sam rolled his shoulders. "I don't know. What I do know is that they're pretty insistent on all of this." He waved his hands around as if showing off the scenery. "And they're all on the same page. I can't get one of them to budge on this insane story they're telling. You know how hard it is to get people to keep their story 100 percent the same from one person to another? Much less three middle-school kids? If they're lying, about any of this, they're doing better than most adults would at keeping their story straight."

"Good point," Billy said. "I hadn't thought of that."

Billy suddenly started looking around, as if there were instant credibility to all of it.

"Yeah. It's probably nothing. Still...come on, we need to catch up."

The kids were already near the top of the steps. The bodyguards hurried to meet them.

"So," Sam said, huffing for air, "which one is the castle?"

Corin glanced down at her phone and then pointed down a narrow street. "Technically, it's a fortress. But that should be it."

"All the way over there?" Sam asked. He heard Billy sigh in frustration. The other guard was a little heavier around the midsection. Not overweight, necessarily, just not as fit as Sam.

"Yep," Corin confirmed with another look at the map she'd pulled up on her phone. "That's the one."

She started walking with the two boys in tow.

Sam glanced at Billy. "Sure you don't want to wait with the car?"

Billy cocked his head to the side and shrugged. "Yeah, maybe I will. Not as spry as I used to be."

Sam slapped him on the back and took off. "Back in a bit. Get yourself a coffee or something."

"Yeah. Yeah." Billy waved his hand in irritation and then turned to walk back down the steps.

Sam caught up with the three friends and tucked in behind them. The group meandered through the serpentine streets, noting the clothing shops, cafés, souvenir stores, and restaurants along the way. Most of the people they passed smiled politely. Only a few seemed focused so intently on something else that they didn't welcome the visitors to their little piece of the world.

"This place sure is old," Sam commented as he looked around, taking in the town. The street was little more than a wide sidewalk paved with smooth, round stones that looked like they might have been around during the time of Caesar. Homes and apartments surrounded them on all sides, towering four and sometimes five stories into the air. While the structures weren't huge by any stretch, they made it feel like the group was walking through an artificial canyon.

He'd felt that way whenever he walked through Manhattan, albeit on a much bigger scale.

Corin stayed in the front, working her way between oncoming pedestrians with a deftness that would have befitted a professional figure skater. The boys bumped into random people more than once as they began their climb up the gradually sloping street.

A bell tower loomed over the buildings up ahead. On the hour, it started chiming out the time.

"So," Sam said, deciding it was as good a time as any to strike up a conversation to pass the time, "what are you guys really up to? Huh? What's so special about this area? I mean, don't get me wrong, it's really old. Seems like a great place to get a cup of coffee and hit up a bakery, but that's kind of most of this country, isn't it?"

Corin answered without looking back. "The Orsini family owned the property where the Pompey Theater was."

"Riiight." Sam elongated the vowel. "We covered that. And you think they might have taken something from the theater."

"Yes."

"And you think that whatever they might have taken could be here, at some museum in a castle?"

"Correct."

"Sounds like a wild goose chase to me."

"Maybe it is."

"Not that you'd believe us anyway," Desmond interjected into their conversation.

Sam rolled his eyes. He couldn't believe he was actually even having this conversation. "When you get older, kid, you'll understand."

"Maybe I don't want to get older if I'm never going to believe people."

It was a harsh little barb, and one that Sam struggled to ignore.

He'd grown up in a decent home. Both of his parents had loved him but were very strict. He wasn't allowed to engage with many creative endeavors, instead being steered in the direction of sports and other physical activities. His father was a football coach. His mother a teacher. They always encouraged him to do his best with education and with athletics, like millions of other parents did.

Sam, though, sometimes felt like he'd missed out on a childhood of wonder, imagination, and adventure. He'd have been lying if he said not even a little part of him was curious about whatever these three were up to. That didn't mean he was willing to do anything that would cost him the easiest job he'd ever had in life. Working for the Ellerbys wasn't a dream job, but it paid well and they respected him, treating him like one of the family. Most of the time it didn't feel like work. As he thought about it, he realized that at this very moment it didn't feel like work, either.

Sam didn't argue Desmond's point. The kid wasn't wrong.

"How do you know what you're looking for at this...museum?" he asked, changing the subject back to the reason they were there.

Desmond's shoulders rose and fell quickly. "Don't know."

"We assume," Diego jumped in after his long silence, "it will look like the last clue we found."

"Which was?"

"A fragment of stone. It had an engraved message on it, written in Latin."

"Like the piece of paper you took to the church."

The kids slowed their pace and exchanged puzzled glances. Had they told him that? How did he know?

Corin picked up her speed again and kept moving.

"The paper wasn't one of the clues. We made a copy in case anything happened to the stone."

"Right." His tone was sarcastic, but he made a mental note. "That was smart," he said quickly to wipe away any sense that he didn't believe their story, even though he still wasn't fully on board.

They made their way past a couple of street performers who were busy juggling soccer balls with their heads and feet. A small crowd of a dozen or so visitors were circled around the two guys as they performed their tricks to the sound of clapping and amazement.

It took the group another ten minutes to reach the fortress entrance. The place was unspectacular with a beige façade, four windows across the second floor, and a bit of stone trimming the corners and doorways. The three entrances were small in comparison to the rest of the structure, two of which were closed with antique iron gates. It was unlikely that the metal barriers were original, but most things weren't when it came to historic locations. Decades and centuries wore down human creations, requiring constant maintenance and renovation.

In some ways, the shape of the building reminded Sam of the Alamo in San Antonio. An eerie feeling crept into the back of his mind along with a disturbing thought. He hoped their visit didn't end the way the last battle at the Alamo had. He snapped his head to shake off the ridiculous notion. There wasn't going to be a fight here, much less any kind of tragedy.

The kids stopped short on the sloped stone path leading up to the ticket office. They were surprised that it didn't have a long line to gain entry.

"This place is really old," Diego said. "I wonder why the line is so short."

"It's a big country," Sam said. "Full of ancient history for tourists to see and explore. Not to mention that this location is a little off the beaten path. Visitors who come here must have done a little research. That, or they're trying to go to the less mainstream places to avoid the crowds."

They walked over to the ticket office and stopped. Corin and the other two looked up at their babysitter with expectant eyes.

"What?" Sam asked, putting his hands out wide. "Oh, you want me to pay for your tickets?"

"We're kids," Corin said. Her tone attempted to make it seem like it should have been obvious. "We don't have jobs or money?"

"Oh, right." Sam made the joke like he didn't know any of that and then reached into his front pocket, pulling out the black leather wallet he usually kept there.

He asked the woman how much, speaking his best Italian. She answered, and he counted out the euros she required for four tickets.

"Where's Billy?" Desmond asked, only now realizing that the other guard wasn't tagging along.

"He stayed with the car," Sam answered as he started passing out the tickets.

"Doesn't he get bored doing that?"

"Maybe." Sam shrugged and turned toward the open gate. "It's part of the job. Nowadays we have phones with things that entertain us while we're sitting around for hours on end doing nothing."

"Shouldn't he be paying attention, you know, watching for signs of trouble?" Corin asked.

This girl didn't miss a thing. "He is paying attention," Sam said. "Just...you know..."

"Just not when there isn't real trouble around?" She crossed her arms in an attacking posture.

Sam wasn't made uncomfortable easily, but the girl's stare was doing the trick. "You know, time is slipping away, and we really need to get back to Rome before your parents find out we took you all the way out here."

His unspoken offer of keeping their little mission quiet seemed to soothe Corin's mind.

"Shall we?" He motioned with his hand toward the entrance.

The kids led the way inside a vast courtyard surrounded on all sides by the same stone that had made up the entire village.

Once they were all inside, Sam looked to the right and found a doorway that was marked with the word "Museum" in three languages.

"Over there," he said. "That's the way to the museum."

"Thanks, Captain?" Diego offered and started walking with his friends across the space.

Sam frowned as he quickened his pace to keep up. "Captain?"

"Captain Obvious," Desmond clarified.

Sam bit his lower lip and gave an understanding nod. "Right. Hilarious."

10

S orano

"HE'S COMING BACK," Carl said and slid into the car seat next to his boss. There was panic in his voice.

"What do you mean he's coming back? Which one?"

"The driver," Carl said. "The one who stayed by the car earlier."

Wayne moved the long tubular microphone off the dash and stuffed it in the back seat. The wires were running all over the center console, but he didn't care. He'd been listening to the conversation of the SUV's occupants just before they left the vehicle and walked up the stairs.

"You get anything useful?" Carl asked, motioning with a flick of the head toward the microphone.

"No," Wayne said. He crouched down low and watched as the driver of the SUV climbed down the steps and walked back over to the vehicle. The guy looked around for a second before getting into the driver's seat and closing the door.

"He didn't see us," Wayne said with confidence.

"That was close."

"Indeed. Did you find anything useful?"

Carl shook his head. "I didn't have time. They'd locked their doors."

"Which you know how to pick."

"Right. I do. I can break into almost any vehicle."

That much was true. It was one of the defining reasons Wayne had brought Carl on in the first place. It was also a reason he'd kept Carl around for so long. He was an artist when it came to picking locks and gaining access to restricted places. All of that made Wayne wonder what the problem was.

"So, why didn't you?"

Carl pointed at the SUV. "Because that guy was coming back. I was just about to do my thing when I caught a glimpse of them at the top of the steps. He was talking to the other guard. Then he gave a nod and started coming back down. I didn't even have time to get my tools out."

That made sense. Carl was lucky he hadn't been spotted, but being on the near side of the vehicle had kept him from view for the most part. It certainly could have been worse. If he'd been seen, the jig would have been up. The SUV driver would have called back to his partner, and before Wayne knew it, the cops would have swarmed the place and had them surrounded. No, Carl did the right thing to hurry back. The fact that the driver was sitting in his SUV actually gave Wayne hope.

The two guards were separated now. Taking them both out at one time would have proved difficult, to say the least. Now, however, one was with the kids up in the castle, while this one was all alone. Wayne half wondered if the guy was sleeping in the driver's seat. It wouldn't have surprised him.

"How you want to handle this, boss?" Carl broke the silence.

Wayne didn't get irritated this time. He had to make a decision. Actually, it had already been made. They would take out the driver first and then go after the other one. When, he didn't know for sure.

An all-out attack in the museum would raise alarms. Cops would show up within minutes despite the remote location. The town surely had a police force of some kind, though Wayne hadn't seen any now that he thought about it.

"We tie him up. Give him a little dose of some sleepy medicine I brought in the bag back there." Wayne pointed into the back seat with his thumb. "Then we wait for the others to come back. When they do, we pounce. You take the guard. I'll round up the kids. Once we have them, they'll have to give us whatever they've got. The map, the clues, everything."

"Good plan."

"Yes, but we have to eliminate that guard first. Grab the duffel bag out of the back. It's got rope in it. Take one of the tranquilizer guns in the back seat. I'll distract the driver while you sneak up on the other side. Pop him with one round of that tranquilizer, and he'll be out for several hours. That should buy us more than enough time."

"Roger that, boss." Carl opened the car door and walked around to the trunk, or boot, as he and Wayne called it.

He took out the duffel bag and unzipped it a few inches to make sure the rope was still in there. It was. Why wouldn't it be? The thing wouldn't up and walk off. Then he opened the back door and grabbed the tranquilizer gun out of another bag, stuffing it into the one with the rope. He slung the bag over his shoulder and started up the sidewalk toward the parked SUV.

Wayne got out of the car and crossed the street. They'd need to approach the target vehicle from different angles so the bodyguard behind the wheel didn't get suspicious as two strangers approached.

Wayne put on his best tourist face, looking around at the buildings and shops with wide eyes, as if he'd never been to Europe before. It was a distant, vaguely ignorant expression that he'd seen millions of times before, both growing up in the UK and on his travels.

Normally, it was the Americans who had that look. They were so engrossed in their own country's culture it was easy to forget how different the rest of the world was. Wayne had seen that look on their faces in other places, not just in Europe. Anywhere he went, it was easy to pick out American tourists.

In a country that was so young and where everything was new and changing, going to a place where homes and churches were more than five hundred years old had to be a shock.

That was the look Wayne wore on his face, a look of pleasant surprise bordering on shock.

He meandered up the sidewalk, only risking a glance across the street at his partner every ten seconds or so as Carl made his way toward the SUV, flanking it from the right.

As Wayne drew near, he noticed the window was open on the driver's side of the SUV. He wasn't sure at first, but it looked like the passenger side was open as well. That would make things considerably easier. Carl could poke his weapon right through the open window and pop the driver with the tranquilizer without having to worry about somehow getting the guy to roll down the window.

Wayne wondered if his luck was finally starting to change.

He reached the end of the sidewalk and watched as Carl looped around behind the SUV, doing his best to look inconspicuous, which only made him look more conspicuous. For someone with his training and expertise, Carl was pretty much an idiot.

Wayne sighed. "Just look like a tourist," he muttered through his teeth.

Carl twisted his head and looked up at a building as if admiring its architecture.

"That's better," Wayne said, as if the guy had heard his initial comment.

Wayne scanned the street in both directions and then crossed, making his way over to the SUV.

"Excuse me," he said, swiveling his head both ways to make sure no other cars were approaching. He knew there weren't, but the gesture served the purpose of making him look naïve. "Sorry to bother you, but may I ask you a question?"

The guy behind the wheel perked up. He'd been staring at his smartphone. Maybe he was reading a novel. Perhaps he was on social media, though Wayne doubted that. Guys in his profession didn't get on social media. They were paranoid about who knew their identities. It was also a way to protect client identities, or at least who the security guys worked for. Anonymity, in the world of private security, was definitely advantageous.

"Yes?" Billy hung one arm out the window. He looked casual, which meant Wayne was playing his role perfectly. The bodyguard didn't appear to be concerned. Perfect.

"I'm terribly sorry," Wayne continued as he approached, "I can't seem to find the castle around here. I heard there's a good one in this town, but I don't feel like walking around all day in this heat to find it." He wiped imaginary sweat from his brow with his forearm and let out a dramatic exhale as if he'd just finished hiking up a mountain.

"Sure, no problem. I'm not actually from around here," Billy explained. "But I have a friend that went to the fortress, castle, whatever. He headed that way a few minutes ago. I think you just go up those stairs and then follow the signs. You should be able to see the building when you're up there. Better vantage point than down here."

"Thank you so much, sir. I can't tell you how much I appreciate your help."

Now where in the world is Carl? Wayne fought off the natural instinct to frown at his assistant's incompetence. He was about to ask another question, hoping the bodyguard didn't suddenly grow suspicious of his lingering. Then Carl appeared on the other side of the SUV with the black tranquilizer gun drawn. He poked it through the window, aiming at the driver's neck.

"No problem," Billy said.

Wayne gave a curt nod and started to walk away. The truth was, he was merely moving clear of the weapon as Carl pulled the trigger. A misfire or errant shot could have rendered Wayne unconscious. There was no poor shot from Carl, though. Wayne heard the gun puff. Then he turned back to see the driver grasping at his neck. The man's face bulged and flushed red. He reached for a weapon in his jacket, but Wayne returned to the door in an instant and grabbed the bodyguard's right hand with both of his. He held the guy's wrist tight until he felt the muscles start to weaken. Within forty-five seconds, the driver was out cold; his head slumped over to one shoulder in a deep sleep.

"He's out," Wayne said and let go of the arm. "Well done, Carl. Now, let's move him in the back and wait for the others to return. When they do, we spring our trap."

11

S orano

CORIN WALKED SLOWLY, just ahead of the others. The museum presented them with a cornucopia of various artifacts from the town's past. Most of the objects and articles had been remarkably preserved. The period clothing was one of the most impressive pieces to the exhibit. Some of the fabrics were original, though there were a few that were clearly replicas made to look like the ones worn so long ago during medieval times.

The group moved along slowly, taking in as much as they could of what the museum had to offer. They didn't want to risk missing something important. There would only be one chance at this. If they screwed up, there was no doubt Sam wouldn't let them come back, and the rest of the vacation to Italy would be more than boring for the three children.

Individually, they all imagined the scenario, but it looked the same to all three.

They'd be resigned to doing the normal tourist stuff, which was fine for Corin and Diego in some regards. They'd never been to Europe before this and certainly hadn't planned on getting into some wild treasure hunt. That was a happy accident that was now turning into a stressful situation.

Corin tried not to think about it as she wove her way through the rows of display cases and a few pillars that held busts, clothing, and tools from the long-ago past.

They were nearing the ninety-minute mark of their investigation, and everything was starting to look the same. If she didn't know better, she'd have sworn they had already come into this part of the museum. She knew that wasn't the case. The artifacts and clothing in here were ones she'd not seen yet.

Still, there was no sign of the stone fragment.

"You three have about thirty minutes left," Sam said after checking his watch.

The kids nodded, though they looked both nervous and concerned. They knew the deal when they came in here. It wasn't like Sam was trying to take advantage of them or ruin their plans. As far as they could tell, he still didn't believe what they'd told him. That part was sort of humorous considering they'd been completely truthful about everything. It must have all sounded so outlandish to an adult that there was nothing he could do to make himself believe it.

Only one thing would change that. Maybe two things. If the two bad guys showed up again, then Sam would know the truth. The kids hoped that scenario wouldn't be played out. They had no desire to be forced into a dangerous situation again.

Yet here they were sneaking around in a museum, looking for the second clue to a treasure each one of them hoped still existed, or hadn't been found yet. That was another topic that continued plaguing their minds: What if the treasure had been dug up by some random person long ago. The world was getting smaller every day. People were building new houses, digging up land, cutting through forests. If Caesar really had hoped to find a treasure somewhere in

Italy or the surrounding area, it very well could have been found by accident, thus rendering their mission a complete waste of time.

Corin shook off the thought and kept going, making her way over to a desk in the far corner of an exhibit room. The desk was huge: at least six feet long, a little over three feet wide, and probably six inches over three feet tall. The wood looked dense and heavy, most likely oak, though the kids didn't really care or desire to study the different types of wood that were used in making furniture. All they knew was that the desk was pretty. Its surface was stained a dark walnut brown. It bore a few scratches, a couple situated on the intricately carved designs cut into the front-facing façade.

"This is a beautiful desk," Corin said. She nearly reached out her hand to run her fingers along it but remembered she was in a museum and likely being watched. For all she knew, an alarm would go off if she touched anything.

"Indeed," Sam said as he and the other two joined her in the corner. "Now, what do you guys say we get out of here and go get some grub? I'm sure Billy is hungry, and we can all find a pizza place around here somewhere."

"You do realize that the pizza here isn't like what we get back home, right?" Diego asked.

"I'm sure you'll think it's delicious."

"Probably way better than the stuff we get in America."

It wasn't Sam's first trip to Italy. He'd been multiple times before and sampled the pizza each time. He loved it, his favorite being from Naples. Sam nodded at the young boy.

"It is."

The others gathered around the desk while Corin inspected it. Desmond yawned and stretched his arms.

"Orsini family desk," he said, looking at the metal plaque that indicated what they were looking at. The placard hung on the wall directly above the desk.

"This must have sat in their castle for generations," Diego said. "Look at the design."

"Clearly from the Renaissance," Corin confirmed. "This thing is definitely old."

"Is this what you three were looking for?" Sam asked. "An antique desk?"

"No." Corin shook her head. She bent her lower back and leaned down, looking underneath the desk then around the edges.

"Then why the interest?" Sam crossed his arms, confused as to why the kids would care about this particular piece of old furniture.

"Maybe there's a secret compartment or something."

The two boys joined in the analysis, checking every seam, every carved relief along the front and sides. While the desk was certainly a tribute to the impeccable craftsmanship of its maker, they found no hidden compartment.

After nearly five minutes of searching, Corin gave up and continued through a doorway that led into the next room.

The others followed her, albeit reluctantly. They'd been in the museum a long time now. If they hadn't found what they were looking for, odds were it wasn't going to be there. Time, it seemed, was running out.

Diego glanced at a map attached to the wall near the doorframe and noted that there was only this room and one other remaining on their tour. He didn't bring it up, thinking it might cause the others to panic or do something rash, like try to go back through the entire museum all over again.

They didn't have time for something like that.

The display cases in the new room were filled with all manner of medieval weaponry. From swords, spears, and knives, to shields, bows, and arrows, it contained an extensive collection of tools of war that were common during the era when the fortress was actively used by the Orsini family.

More swords hung from the wall, in order of oldest to most recently created. Huge shields hung close to many of them, each with the family coat of arms emblazoned across the front.

Corin split off from the others and walked along a row of display cases that showed off smaller weapons. Desmond took to a middle row, doing the same, though he walked a little faster as he realized there was nothing like what they were looking for.

Diego took the row to the left of the entry and studied each piece with interest as he moved quietly from one display box to the next.

Sam stood in the middle of the doorway with his arms crossed. He glanced down at his watch, hoping that somehow time would tick by faster. His patience with this entire "treasure hunt" was running out. The one piece of hope that kept him from losing his mind was that for the rest of the trip these brats would have to do whatever he said. No more running around. No more chasing made-up stories about ancient treasures.

He'd only been in Rome for a few days, and already Sam felt like he needed a vacation. The irony wasn't lost on him. These three *were* here for a vacation. When it was all over, Sam would get a week or two off. That's how it always was when the Ellerbys did something like this. They'd be in Rome for two to three weeks and then head back to the States. When they did, there would be a few weeks to a month where they didn't do anything except paperwork, online interviews, and begin their search for the next big discovery.

Sam loved those times. They still paid him a retainer fee, which was more than generous on their part. He made sure to always express sincere appreciation for that. Now, more than ever, he craved that off time. Even though it would be a couple of weeks until he reached that point, once they were back in Rome things would slow down again, and he could resume normal babysitting duties instead of traipsing all over the country.

"Guys?" Diego's voice abruptly cut through the deathly silence of the museum. "I think I found it."

The other two kids snapped their heads around and then rushed over to where their friend was standing, staring into one of the display cases.

Sam's heart sank. *Oh, come on,* he thought. There couldn't really be something there. Right?

He trudged over to where the kids were eagerly looking through the glass. They refrained from tapping on it, though Sam could tell that's exactly what each one of them was pining to do.

Sam rounded the corner of the case and followed their gazes into the box. On the top shelf was a piece of stone. The edges were cut clean, as if done with modern tools, with almost laser precision. A sequence of letters he didn't recognize was carved into the stone.

"What is that?" Sam asked. He wished he hadn't the second the words escaped his lips.

"It's the stone we've been looking for," Desmond said. His voice trembled with excitement, like a kid who'd just unwrapped a new bicycle for their birthday.

"Okay, I think we've gone through enough of this little game you three have been playing. It's just a piece of rock."

"No, it's not," Desmond insisted.

"He's right," Corin agreed. "We need this stone. It's the second piece to the puzzle that leads to Caesar's treasure."

Sam rolled his eyes. Not this again.

"Guys. How many times do I have to tell you? There is no treasure. Okay? I don't know what the three of you are getting at, but I'm tired of it. We're leaving."

"No, please." Desmond begged now, grasping at Sam's suit jacket. "We have to find the curator."

Sam saw the sincerity in Desmond's eyes. There was no deceit there. Only desperation. Sam sighed.

"Look, kid. Let's say you're not making all this up and that rock really is a part of a big treasure map that leads to some ancient stash of gold somewhere. It's not like they're gonna let us take it when we go. That thing is part of this museum. Honestly, it's part of this town's history. It belongs here."

The kids lowered their heads, suddenly dejected. Desmond turned and gazed into the box once more. They were so close.

"I have an idea," Corin blurted.

The boys perked up.

"Yeah?" Diego asked.

She nodded and took the phone out of her pocket, tapped on the camera app, and then tilted the screen until it was lined up with the stone centered perfectly on the screen.

"Hey, you can't take pictures in here," Sam said.

"There aren't any signs saying we can't." Desmond argued.

Sam gasped, frustrated. "We passed them on the way in. They explicitly said visitors are not permitted to take flash photography."

Corin chuckled. "I'm not using the flash."

She tapped the button and then adjusted her angle, repeating the process three times until she had images from multiple views on her phone.

"What are you thinking?" Diego asked. "Those pictures won't help us fill in the gap meant for that stone on the map."

"Don't worry," she said. "I have a plan."

12

S orano

THE GROUP STRODE quickly out of the museum. Sam was still trying to understand what was going on as he did his best to keep the kids at a respectable place.

"Guys," he pleaded, "slow down. We can't run through a museum like this."

The kids obeyed and slowed to a brisk walk, though more than once he had to remind them not to push it.

"What has got you three so excited all of a sudden?" Sam asked.

"We'll tell you outside," Corin responded without looking back at him.

They passed through the exit and waved politely to the lady behind the counter at the gift shop. When they were back out in the courtyard just beyond the entrance to the castle, Corin hurried over to a bench under a shady tree and sat down. She scrolled through the pictures on her phone for a moment, making sure the ones she'd taken were good enough for what she had in mind.

The boys sat down on either side of her, leaning in to get a better view.

"Those look good," Desmond said. "But I still don't get how we're going to fill in the gap with the puzzle."

"Yeah," Sam said, as if he knew what they were talking about. "And I'm still wondering what is going on. Would you mind filling me in here?" He threw his hands out in a dramatic show of exasperation.

"We tried to tell you," Diego said. "But you wouldn't listen to us. You thought we were lying."

Sam's head bobbed as he turned it one way and then the other. He was at his wit's end.

"Okay, fine. You're right. Okay? You're all correct. I didn't believe you. I still don't know what all this is about, so there's a part of me that still doesn't believe you. It would be helpful if someone would let me know what is going on around here because, quite frankly, it's making me a little crazy!"

His voice rose, and the kids collectively leaned back for a second as he finished his rant.

Then they giggled.

"You really look funny when you get angry," Corin commented and then went back to looking at her phone.

"I'm not angry!" Sam realized he was yelling and lowered his voice. "I'm not angry," he said in a much quieter tone. "I'm just frustrated."

The kids exchanged glances with each other and then looked back up at the bodyguard.

"We told you before," Desmond said. "We're looking for an ancient treasure. Yes, we know it might not be there anymore, like you said. But we've found two pieces of the puzzle that will show us the location."

"Pieces?" Sam said. He was calming down, and his breathing was no longer fast like he'd been running. "You mean that piece of rock back there with the...what was it you said?"

"Latin inscription." The three kids said the words together.

"Right." Sam's voice sounded absent, bewildered. "So...that piece of rock. It goes with another rock?"

The kids nodded.

"And that other rock is where?"

"In the hotel," Corin said.

"Okay. And what about the map?"

"It's there, too," Diego answered.

"And before you ask," Desmond chimed in again, "the pieces fit over the map. There are three of them. When we have all three pieces, the stones will show us where the treasure is on the map."

Sam's head went up and down, but they could tell he was still having a hard time believing them.

"Look, we'd love for you to be a part of this, Sam. You've been very cool about bringing us up here today and letting us look around. Now we've found the second piece to this puzzle of keys, but we don't speak Latin."

"No?"

The kids shook their heads.

"Then how did you know what the first stone said? Huh?" He posed like he finally had them caught in a web of lies.

"We spoke to a priest at the church you took us to."

"Yeah," Corin agreed. "Remember how I went in to the confession booth?"

Sam's face went pale as he realized they had an explanation for the only tough question he could conjure. "A priest?"

"Yeah," Diego said. "We met him the other night. That's how we figured out the first clue. Then he gave Corin the translation for the riddle on the first keystone."

Sam licked his top lip and turned his head, looking out over the town from the slightly higher vantage point. The beige buildings were cradled by two ridges of rolling green hills.

He turned back and faced them with a resolute gaze. "Okay, then. I believe you."

Each one of the kids raised their eyebrows in surprise.

"You do?" Desmond asked.

"Sure. Why not? There's buried treasure all over this planet. Your parents have proved that."

"Well, they technically look for artifacts and relics, not treasure." Desmond offered the correction with a sheepish grin.

"Yeah, fine. Artifacts. Whatever. One man's trash and all that."

"They're not trash."

"You know what I mean. Beauty's in the eye of the beholder? Sayings?"

The kids shook their heads and started laughing at how frazzled the imposing bodyguard was.

"You're kind of silly sometimes. You know that?" Diego asked.

Sam fought off the urge to chuckle. "Fine. I'm silly. Let's just go with I believe you and will help if you want me to. Okay? Doesn't look like I'm going to get out of that anyway."

He took another quick look out over the valley. "What's the next move, then? You obviously can't get that rock out of the museum. You said you had a plan." He directed the last statement to Corin.

She nodded, suddenly excited again. "Yes. So, we can't get the stone, right?"

The others bobbed their heads in agreement.

"I was looking at the shape of it, and I realized that it's not cut jagged."

Her brother looked confused. "So? What does that mean?"

"The keystones were cut clean."

"Really clean," Desmond added.

"Right. So, I got to thinking, if we could get back to the hotel, I can create a 3-D model in one of my applications."

"How will that help?" Sam asked. His eyebrows knit together.

"Once I have a 3-D rendering of the keystone, I can upload it to a 3-D printer."

The two boys' eyes lit up as they realized what she had in mind.

"The printed model will fit just as well as the real thing."

"Exactly."

"Printed model?" Sam asked. "Where you gonna get a 3-D printer in Rome?"

"The museum where my parents' exhibit is should have one," Desmond said. "They have all kinds of cool lab equipment there. I say once we have the 3-D rendering on an SD drive, we run over there and take a look around. I'm sure the curator won't mind."

Sam thought about it for a minute before he said anything. "It'll have to wait until tomorrow. It's a little over a two-hour drive back, and by the time we arrive in Rome it will be time for dinner. Your parents will be expecting us. They'll also want to know what we did all day."

A look of dread cascaded over the kids' faces.

"What are you going to tell them?" Desmond asked.

Sam's shoulders rose and fell once. "The truth. I'm gonna tell them we went up to an old castle north of the city and drove around the countryside a little bit, taking in the sights and learning about the area's history."

The kids' faces instantly transitioned to relief.

"Thanks, Sam," Desmond said.

"No problem, kid." He reached out and tousled Desmond's hair. Then his expression changed to one of worry. "Oh, no. I forgot about Billy. He's probably been sitting there in the car for the last few hours."

"Maybe he fell asleep," Diego offered.

Sam chuckled. "He'd better not have. We don't get paid to sleep on the job. Come on. Let's get back to the car. I don't want you three to be late for dinner."

The four hurried down the sloped street and back onto the main path that cut through the city on the hill. There was a renewed energy in their step, causing them to almost break out at a jog more than once.

The possibility that they'd be able to replicate the second keystone sent thrills through them. Even Sam seemed to be, at the very least, curious regarding the whole thing, which was better than the utter disbelief he displayed before.

They reached the top of the steps and looked down at the parking area. The SUV was exactly where they left it. They saw the suited figure sitting in the driver's seat and waved. Billy didn't wave back. From the looks of it, he was holding his phone, but they couldn't really see his face through the tinted window on the right and because of where the roof met the windshield.

The group carefully made their way back down the steps to the parking area and strolled toward the vehicle. The kids were only ten feet away from it when Sam realized something was wrong. Billy would have seen them coming and gotten out of the car to open a door or two. Instead he was sitting there, still looking down at his phone. The visor over the steering wheel was pulled down to keep his face shaded, but it made seeing his head impossible from their angle.

Sam slowed his pace. "Billy?" he said. Sam hesitated and then saw movement from the driver. There was something...different about him.

"That's far enough, old boy." The accented voice cut through the oddly silent parking area.

Sam spun around, reaching for his weapon, but it was too late.

He came face to face with Wayne Collins, who held a strange-looking pistol in his right hand. Its barrel was leveled at Sam's gut.

Wayne clicked his tongue and shook his head. "Uh-uh-uh." He wagged a warning finger with his free hand. "You won't be needing that weapon."

The kids spun around at the sound of the familiar voice. Their eyes filled with fear.

Diego yelled. Corin screamed. Desmond started to run toward Sam as if he had some power to save the bodyguard. A hand clapped down on Desmond's shoulder, suddenly halting his forward momentum.

"Where do you think you're going?" It was the guy from the driver's side of the vehicle. He'd gotten out when the kids were distracted by Wayne. Now he had Desmond by the collar and had wrapped one arm around Corin's neck, holding her tight in a bear hug.

"Sam!" Desmond said, being dragged back.

Diego froze. He was the only one that hadn't been caught, but he was paralyzed with fear.

Sam spun around and saw the trouble the three kids were in. Then he turned back to the man with the tranquilizer gun. "Let them go. They're just kids."

A sickening laugh escaped Wayne's lips, the sound slithering between his teeth.

"No," Wayne said. His head turned slowly from one side to the other. "No, I don't think so. They have something I need."

Sam did his best acting job, putting on a confused scowl. "They don't have anything. Look at them."

Wayne risked a quick glance beyond Sam and assessed the children. They didn't have any bags with them, and at first glance their pockets appeared empty, save for the familiar bulge a mobile phone imprinted on pants and jeans.

"Doesn't look like they have anything except their phones, boss," Carl confirmed, holding on to Desmond as he struggled to get free. "Stop wriggling, you little brats."

Diego was still free, though standing motionless, almost as if not moving would somehow make him invisible.

Wayne peered at them through slits for eyes. "What did you do with it?"

"What are you talking about?" Sam asked, trying to keep the conversation and the attention focused on him instead of the kids. "What did you do with Billy?"

"You be quiet." Wayne wagged the gun threateningly at the bodyguard. "Where did you put the stone, kids? Huh? I know you found it at the temple where you left Carl and me in the cold, dark muck. Well, now it's going to get very cold where you three are going. What do you think, Carl? Leave them in a murky ditch somewhere outside town?"

"If you lay a finger on them," Sam said.

"You'll do what?" Wayne turned back to the bodyguard standing between himself and the kids. "I already knocked out your partner.

He's asleep in the back of the SUV. Don't worry, you'll be joining him soon. You all will."

Wayne raised the weapon, making sure the sights were squarely lined up on Sam's chest. "Don't worry," Wayne snarled. "I'm not going to permanently hurt them. Once we have what's ours, we'll be on our way."

"It's not yours," Corin blurted. "That treasure belongs in a museum!"

"Oh, how very noble of you," Wayne sneered. "It belongs in a museum." He mocked her high-pitched voice.

"That treasure is mine. And I want to know where the stone is. That is somehow connected to all this."

"Yeah," Carl voiced. "We also want to know why you three came all the way up here."

Wayne rolled his eyes. It was true. They'd wondered why the group traveled two hours north of Rome yet appeared to be empty-handed. "Yes," Wayne said, reluctant to agree with his assistant. "Why did you come up here?"

Diego had stood still long enough. Crippled by fear, he'd been unable to force himself to do anything to help his sister and friend. Now, however, the men seemed focused on their reason for being in Sorano. The gunman didn't aim his weapon away from Sam, which was a problem if he pulled the trigger. Diego didn't know the gun was a tranquilizer; not that it mattered. An unconscious Sam would still leave them stuck there, two hours away from Rome—and Desmond's parents.

Diego spun around and faced the guy holding Desmond and his sister. "Let them go," he said. His voice quivered as he desperately pushed fear out of the way and summoned every ounce of courage he could.

Corin and Desmond looked just as surprised as their captor.

"What did you just say, boy?" Carl hissed.

"Shut him up," Wayne ordered. "I asked you a question."

"Last chance," Diego said, taking a step toward Carl.

The man pinched his eyebrows together and laughed, like he would at a threat from an ant.

"You should have run away, boy."

"Maybe," Diego said.

Carl let go of Corin for a second, snatching out at Diego's neck to grab him and pull him into the fold. Diego deftly ducked his head to the side, the fingers narrowly missing his throat. He surged forward and kicked as hard as he could, driving the top of his foot into the zipper of Carl's pants.

A shriek escaped the man's lips, and his grip on Desmond instantly weakened.

Desmond and Corin spun around, now free from their wrangler's hands.

Carl groaned and grabbed at his lap, desperately hoping gravity would ease his pain. Before he could find relief, Desmond and Corin kicked him hard in the shins with the tips of their shoes, sending a new sharp pain up through Carl's legs.

The guy dropped to the ground, writhing in agony.

Wayne turned his attention to the unexpected attack from the children. The gun followed his eyes. His finger tensed on the trigger, ready to deliver a tranquilizer dart into Diego's arm.

Before he could get off a shot, Sam rushed him and barged his shoulder into Wayne's chest.

The villain tumbled backward, and the gun clacked on the pavement. Wayne tripped over his heel and fell onto his back. Sam kicked the gun across the pavement, sending it sliding thirty feet away. He was about to jump on Wayne when he heard Desmond shout his name.

"Sam, come on!"

The bodyguard saw the crumpled man next to the SUV. The kids were already climbing in the back seat.

"Oh, great," Sam muttered. He looked back at Wayne, who was scrambling to get to his feet.

"We'll meet again, Wayne. This isn't over."

Sam turned and sprinted back to the SUV. He could hear the

sound of whining Italian sirens in the distance echoing through the canyon of old buildings.

He flung open the driver's side door and noted the keys were still in the ignition. Wayne and Carl had thought of almost everything. Almost. If they were smart, they'd have taken the keys, too.

Sam turned the key and the engine revved to life.

"Billy's back here," Desmond said, sitting on his knees and looking into the extra seat in the back.

"Okay. Seat belts. We gotta go."

Desmond dropped down onto his bottom and buckled in. The other two were already putting on their seat belts.

Sam shifted the vehicle into drive and whipped the wheel around to the left as Carl staggered to his feet. He looked in the rearview mirror and saw Wayne stumble over to the tranquilizer gun, but they were already out of range, not to mention the darts wouldn't penetrate the SUV's windows or metal body.

He steered the car to the right at the next intersection, and the two British men disappeared from view.

Sam glanced back again, this time at the kids. "You guys okay?" All sense of anger and frustration had disappeared.

"Yeah," Corin said as she finally caught her breath. "We're good."

The boys nodded.

"Were those the two guys you mentioned before?" Sam already knew the answer, but for some reason he needed confirmation.

"Yeah," Desmond said. "Those were the men."

Sam licked his top lip and looked back at the street quickly vanishing behind them. *Wayne Collins and his henchman, Carl,* he thought. That changed everything.

13

S orano

SAM KEPT his foot on the gas as much as he could during the return drive to Rome. The drive that took a little over two hours earlier in the day took about twenty minutes less on the drive back. He had no intention of letting Wayne and Carl catch up to them before they made it to the hotel.

Billy woke up about halfway, rousing from his sleep with a groggy growl. He rubbed his head and groaned, eyelids barely able to lift as if stuck together with some kind of glue.

"What happened?" he asked as he forced himself up in the far rear seat. "My head is killing me."

"Morning, sunshine," Desmond said, turning around to look at the second bodyguard.

"You were shot with a tranq gun," Sam said.

"I was?"

"Yeah. Had a little run-in with Wayne Collins and his troll, Carl."

Billy blinked, his eyelids working faster now. "That's who that was." The realization hit him. "I knew I recognized that guy." Billy shook his head, which only seemed to make the pounding in his skull that much worse. "I guess he surprised me. I didn't see Carl, though."

"Just rest for a few more minutes," Sam said. His voice had a hint of sympathy. "Not sure what drug they used, but you were out for a good couple of hours, assuming you were unconscious most of the time we were in the castle."

"The castle? Oh, right. Did you kids find what you were looking for?" He asked the question like he'd believed them all along.

The kids nodded.

"Oh, that's good." Billy almost toppled over to the side and fell asleep again, but his hand shot out and braced his weight. "Whoa. Still a little woozy."

"We'll fill you in on the details when we get back to Rome."

Billy frowned. "I guess you guys got the best of Wayne and Carl. Sorry I let them get the drop on me."

"We almost didn't get away," Sam said. He slowed down after one more check in the rearview mirror. The two men were nowhere in sight, and the cars following them had mostly turned off the road, replaced by others that were traveling in the same direction, back to Rome.

Sam pieced everything together as quickly as he could before speaking again. "So," he said, "I guess you guys weren't lying after all."

"We tried to tell you," Desmond said.

"Yeah, I know. You gotta understand, though, everything you guys told me...that's not normal stuff for kids to be involved with. Not kids your age, anyway. You could have been hurt, or something worse."

The warning tone in his voice hit them hard. He sounded like he truly cared, not just about his job but also about them.

"Dez," Sam shortened the name, "I've been working for your parents a long time. You're like my own kid. You know that, right?"

Desmond conceded a nod.

"Taking care of you is more than just a job. That goes for Billy back there, too."

Billy gave a semiconscious nod.

"We treat your friends the same way, Dez. It's important that we keep you all safe. If something were to happen to you, any of you, I wouldn't be able to forgive myself. You understand?"

This time, all the kids nodded.

"Okay. Now that we understand each other, you have two options."

"Two options?" Desmond asked. "What do you mean?"

Sam swerved the SUV into the left lane, passing a slower hatchback in the right before merging back into the lane ahead of the other car.

"We got away from Wayne and Carl, sure, but those two are slippery. If they tracked you...us...all the way out here, odds are they'll try again."

"And they'll be mad," Diego added.

Sam fired a surprised glance at the boy and then nodded. "Yeah. They'll be mad."

"They seemed pretty mad today," Corin said.

"No kidding." Billy rubbed his skull.

"My point is," Sam continued, "they'll be back. We can increase security around the hotel, change your rooms, all that, but the bottom line is that if we venture out into the city again or, heaven forbid, the countryside, there's only so much we can do."

"What are you saying, Sam?" Desmond asked.

Sam took in a deep breath. The sun was setting over the hills to the west, making a silhouette out of some ancient ruins that likely were the fragmented remains of a regional king's castle from long ago.

"Option one," Sam said, "is we stay at the hotel for the rest of your visit. There's a swimming pool, activity rooms, a game room, and a lot of places for you to run around without getting into trouble." He glanced back and saw the uncertain expressions on the faces behind him. "Well, at least too much trouble anyway. You three seem to find it around every corner."

"That option doesn't sound good," Desmond said. "We came here to see Rome, to experience the Old World. We don't want to be stuck inside the rest of the time we're here. I doubt my parents would want that, either."

"Right," Sam said. "Plus, if they found out that you three weren't getting out to see the city, they'd wonder why. Eventually, we'd have to tell them everything. I don't like that option."

"Neither do I," Billy moaned from the back.

"I don't think your parents would fire us," Sam said, "but their trust of our handling your care would definitely diminish."

The inside of the vehicle fell silent for a moment as the kids considered what he was saying. Sam was right. If the Ellerbys found out about any of this, their trip would be over. Diego and Corin worried that they'd be sent home early. Desmond pictured doing nothing but spending time with his parents the rest of the time he was in Italy. That didn't sound good, either.

"What's option two?" Corin asked.

Sam's shoulders raised slightly and then drooped again.

"Well, the way I see it, taking care of you three is our top priority. Also, keeping our jobs is important."

"Understandable."

"But we can't very well put you in a room for weeks on end. That means we're going to have to take you out of the building now and then, at least for the sake of appearances."

The three kids glanced at each other with dubious expressions. They weren't sure they liked where this was going.

"So, I think the best option is that Billy and I help you with whatever it is you're trying to find."

He steered the car into the left lane again to pass a delivery truck. Once the slower vehicle was behind them, he merged back to the right once more.

The kids sat in stunned silence. Had they just heard correctly? Was Sam offering to actually help them with this Caesar's treasure mission?

"Wait a second," Desmond said. Suspicion filled his voice. "You're saying that you'll not only not tell my parents about any of this, but you're going to help us, too?"

"Seems like the best way to make sure nothing happens to you three. Like I said, Wayne and Carl will be back. Billy and I will make sure that the cops are on the lookout for them. This isn't the first time Wayne has caused problems with an Ellerby. He's been jealous of your parents for a long time, Dez."

"I got that impression," Desmond said with a grin.

"Well, now it will really get under his skin that the young Ellerby is two steps ahead of him, too. Wayne will be back; that much is certain, but he'll have to be much more careful now that we know he's skulking around."

"Disguises," Diego said. "They'll probably wear disguises."

"Could be," Sam agreed. "Whatever the case, we'll need to keep our eyes peeled for anything and anyone suspicious."

He took a deep breath and exhaled. "Now, we need to know every-thing about what you three are looking for. Start from the beginning. I know you told us some stuff, but let's go over it again, just to make sure I understand what's going on."

Desmond and the other two told the story of how they stum-bled into the vault and climbed up on the ancient boat. Sam cringed at that part. He'd known what happened based on what the kids said before, but it still grated his nerves. He wasn't a history buff, far from an aficionado, but he knew how important it was to maintain structural integrity for something like that ship, or anything else in a museum. Artifacts had to be handled with tremendous care.

The kids continued the story, each sharing a particular part about the events of the previous day and how they narrowly escaped Wayne and Carl's grasp the first time. The harrowing story sent a twist of concern across Sam's face, but he said nothing until they were done telling the tale.

"I'm glad you guys didn't get hurt," Sam said when they were finished. "I don't know if you three realize how dangerous it was to go out on your own."

"In Rome. In the middle of the night." Billy's addition didn't make the kids feel any better. In fact, it made them feel more guilt.

"Sorry, Sam," Desmond offered.

"We are, too," Diego said.

"It's okay. You're fine. Please promise me, no more running away like that again. Okay? I'm just glad your parents didn't find out about that."

He let the gravity of his words linger for another minute.

"So," Desmond said, "does this mean that you're wanting to join up with us?"

Sam let out a sigh. "I don't know how you think this is going to end, but there's no sense in us trying to fight it. We have to let you get out and see Rome, but with Wayne and Carl out there, we'll need to have a plan in place to keep you three safe. If we run into those guys again, I don't think they'll be so slow to act next time."

"Right," Corin said. "Which means we need to be faster."

"Yeah." Sam sounded disappointed.

The kids knew why. His cushy job of watching three middle-schoolers for a few weeks in the summer had just turned into an unexpected adventure, with a real threat of danger on top. "What's the next move? And what is it you're calling your little crew?"

"The Adventure Guild," the kids said as one.

"I like it," Billy said. "Do we get code names?"

Desmond raised an eyebrow and turned around to look at the man. "Um, sure. If you want one."

"Do you guys have them?"

They shook their heads.

"Oh." He sounded dejected. "Never mind then."

"Okay, Adventure Guild," Sam said. "Our next move: We go back to the hotel and have dinner with your parents. Then we make sure the stuff you put in their room is safe and secure. After that, we get a good night's sleep."

"And tomorrow head to the museum to see if they have a 3-D printer?" Hope fluttered in Corin's voice.

"That's right. Billy and I will make sure there isn't anyone lurking around the building in the morning. We'll sneak you three out and head to the museum. It's a safe place. And the security guys should have the bugs worked out with all the cameras. If Wayne and Carl show up there, we'll know about it."

Sam considered what he'd just said and spoke up again. "That reminds me. How did you three do that with the cameras?"

The kids frowned and glanced at each other, genuinely searching for answers.

"You mean you didn't do that to the cameras?"

"Do what?" Diego asked. There was no lie in his eyes.

"The cameras," Sam said. "They weren't working. They were showing the vault, the hallways, all that stuff, but we never saw you three getting on the boat. You were in the security room when we reviewed the footage. How'd you do it?"

"Sam," Desmond cut in, "we didn't do that. Honestly, we were worried the cameras would show everything."

Sam's frown deepened. "That means someone else did it."

"Wayne and Carl?"

"Yeah," Sam nodded. "Well, that explains that. I wasn't entirely convinced you three had the tech know-how to pull off something that advanced."

"Hey!" Corin did her best to sound offended.

Sam chuckled. "No offense. But that kind of scrambling technology takes a good bit of knowledge."

"It's okay. I bet I could learn it quickly, though."

"I'm sure you could."

Something in the back of Sam's mind told him that these three probably could figure out the tech behind the scrambled video signals. They weren't ordinary children. These three were clever, intelligent, and tougher than expected. Wayne and Carl were dangerous, but these kids had gotten the better of them. That in itself was pretty impressive.

Just help them find whatever it is they're looking for, he thought to himself. *Then all this will be over. And hopefully, Wayne and Carl will end up in jail.* Then Sam could relax on a beach somewhere and let go of all his worries, at least for a little while.

He saw a sign that showed how many kilometers it was to Rome. They'd be back in time for dinner at this rate. Sam didn't say it out loud, but he planned on skipping dinner. He was going to have a long night ahead of him to make sure the building was secure. For the moment, Wayne and Carl were still out there. Sam wondered what the two villains would try next.

14

S orano

NEITHER MAN in the car said anything for the first ten minutes of the drive out of the little mountain village.

Carl knew that his boss was angry. The man didn't have to say anything for him to pick up on that. Carl was frustrated, too. In part, he blamed Wayne for taking his eyes off Sam the bodyguard for even one second.

"I cannot believe you let them get away again," Wayne blurted, thus ending the long silence that had filled the sedan.

"Me?" Carl was incensed. "You were the one holding the gun on Sam. Why didn't you just shoot him?"

"What if I missed and hit you? You were standing right behind him with those three little brats. And by the way, speaking of, how in the world did you let those children beat you up, Carl? Huh? That's two times now."

"I didn't see you doing anything to help." He grabbed at his leg where a bruise had developed from being kicked in the shin. "And they're tougher than they look."

Wayne threw up both hands, letting go of the steering wheel for a moment. "They're like, ten years old!"

"I think they're more like twelve or thirteen."

Wayne's blood boiled. His face burned red, and his eyes looked like they might pop out of his face.

"Are you seriously arguing with me about the age of a few kids?" His voice roared. "I don't care if they're eighteen. There is no way in the universe they should be able to get away from the two of us!"

"Agreed. Which is why you should have shot the bodyguard, and then we could have knocked the kids out, too."

Wayne sighed and rubbed his forehead. "Look, Carl. I understand your fervor concerning how to handle this situation, but I have a real issue administering a tranquilizer to three kids, especially shooting them with a dart."

"Really?" Carl was genuinely surprised. "Because I thought you were okay with doing pretty much whatever to them."

"I don't mind slipping them something that might make them sleep, but I don't want to harm the kids. We may be thieves, but we're not sickos. Darting the kids was never the plan. We were going to tie them up and put them in the back of the truck. The tranquilizers were for their bodyguards."

"Fine," Carl said. He almost sounded disappointed. "What's our next move?"

Wayne had been agonizing over that since the second Sam tore off in the SUV with the kids and the other guard. He and Carl had barely made it back to their car in time, narrowly avoiding the police as they arrived on the scene just minutes later.

"They're going back to Rome," Wayne said. His voice cut the silence like a katana through a watermelon.

"Yeah, I figured as much." Carl sounded grumpy.

"That means we're going back to Rome, too."

"Figured that, too." He rested his head on his palm, elbow against the windowsill.

"Problem is, now they'll be spooked."

"Good."

Wayne shook his head and sighed through his nose. "Don't you understand? Now that they know who we are and what we're up to, those bodyguards will have the hotel crawling with cops and security. No way we'll get in there again. Not until the Ellerbys leave."

The inside of the car went silent again. The only sounds that filled the cabin were from the tires on the road, the wind against the side mirrors, and the engine whining.

Wayne racked his brain, fighting against useless emotions as he attempted to come up with a solution to their new problem. Knowing his luck, the bodyguards probably didn't believe the kids when—or if —they told the men about their encounter with him and Carl the previous night. Didn't matter. If they'd kept silent on the issue, the results were still the same. Sam knew what was going on. He knew who Wayne and Carl were, though only as a result of a few random encounters.

They'd crossed paths at least three times that Wayne recalled. No hostilities were ever exchanged save for a few verbal insults. Sam knew about Wayne's jealousy. The wealthy Brit wasn't sure how, but Sam was onto his motives. Maybe he was too obvious.

Whatever the reason, their last conversation—if it could be called that—wasn't a pleasant one. It resulted in Sam having security escort Wayne out of the building where the Ellerbys kept their offices.

Wayne had gone there to see if they'd be interested in part-nering up on a project, one he'd realized was a dead end without their help. They'd respectfully declined. Wayne had disrespectfully protested. Sam and the other security guards removed him from the property.

Up to the point where Wayne had snuck into the museum during the Ellerbys' Roman exhibit, he'd never really broken any laws. Bent some? Sure. But criminal activity wasn't his bag. At least it hadn't been. The frustration boiling inside of him was quickly changing that.

He found his mind not only wandering to criminal solutions for this current problem, but zipping to them instantly, bypassing appropriate and legal means of getting what he wanted.

He still had no intentions of hurting the children, though that sentiment was waning as well. Those little kids were a problem, a thorn in his side. He'd only dealt with them twice now, and they'd somehow managed to outsmart him each time.

Carl was little help. After this was all over, Wayne would let him go. He didn't have a care in the world what Carl did after that. They weren't exactly friends. Sure, Carl had been unquestioningly loyal for a few years now, but that didn't matter. He was a hired gun, a henchman. When he was gone, Wayne figured Carl would have no problem finding work with someone else. And if he didn't, Wayne couldn't care less.

"So, there's no way we can get into their hotel." Carl was thinking out loud. "And if we try to follow them, they'll know it."

"Which means we have to do things differently from now on."

"What do you mean?"

Wayne tipped his head to the side and raised one eyebrow. "It means we'll have to be more careful, more clever, sneakier."

"How we gonna do that, boss?"

Wayne was still working on the plan, but he recalled something a mentor told him long ago about plans. What was it the person said? Usually, the simplest answer is the correct one? It was something like that. Wayne figured it applied to their current situation.

"We split up," Wayne said after another moment of thought.

"Split up? You sure that's a good idea?"

Wayne nodded. "Yes. In fact, it's necessary. They'll be looking for the two of us together. By splitting up, it will make us harder to track." The plan formulated quickly in Wayne's mind now. He saw everything playing out like a movie in all its brilliant glory.

Carl was trying to follow along, but he wasn't a mind reader. "So, if we split up and try to follow them, they'll still see one of us. No offense, boss, but I don't want to get arrested. I've been in the slammer before. I don't feel like going back."

Wayne knew about Carl's criminal past. He'd done some time for petty little crimes, nothing major. He'd pickpocketed some, shoplifted at a few places, even broke into a business to steal money from a cash register that he believed would be full. It wasn't. That should have been Wayne's clue that Carl wasn't the brightest assistant, but he overlooked it, thinking everyone makes mistakes. That oversight, apparently, had been Wayne's mistake.

"You won't go back, Carl. Don't worry about that." Wayne did his best to soothe the oddly fragile henchman. "This is how it works. We can't get into the hotel, but I doubt they'll have security positioned far from it. We watch and wait. When the kids leave the building, and they will, we follow them."

"Which is when those two bodyguards will see us and call the cops."

"No." Wayne shook his head. "They'll see us following for a few minutes, and then whoever is first will turn off the street. We'll play a shell game with them. Whoever turns off can catch back up a little later, working around through side streets and back roads."

Carl frowned, clearly not fond of the idea. "Okay, I get what you're saying, but what are we supposed to do when they get out of town onto a country road or something? We were lucky they didn't notice us following them here. And then there's the issue that we don't necessarily know they're going to keep looking for this treasure. I mean, what if they just give up and decide not to pursue it anymore? Honestly, if I was that guard, there's no way I'd even allow those kids to leave the hotel again. Would you?"

It was an issue Wayne had considered before his assistant started talking. He didn't have a definitive answer. "It's a risk we'll have to take. We stake out the hotel from a safe distance and watch for those guards to leave. When they do, we'll follow. I don't think those kids are going to walk away from this case now. They're kids, after all. If they think for a second there's any chance they'll be able to find this treasure, there's no way they're quitting. They'll go after it. When they do, this time we'll be ready."

15

R ome

SAM PATIENTLY WEAVED through what was by far some of the most chaotic traffic he'd ever been in during his entire life. Cars were driving haphazardly in the lanes. Motorcycles and scooters drifted between the larger vehicles, dipping in and out of lanes to get a few yards ahead before having to come to a complete stop once more as the stoplights halted progress.

Sam rested his chin on the palm of his left hand with the elbow propped on the doorsill. He sighed for the hundredth time since arriving back in the big city. It was getting dark, so he knew rush hour was long gone. The traffic should have been dispersed by now, or so he thought. Then again, it wasn't *that* late. If he'd been objective about it, he'd have realized that the number of drivers on the road was similar to when the group left the city earlier that day.

He was relieved the trip was over and that they, he hoped,

wouldn't have to go out to Sorano again, or anywhere else for that matter.

Sam glanced into the mirror on the outside of his door, checking again for anyone who might be following them. Specifically, he was looking for Wayne Collins.

Sam remembered Wayne from a few personal encounters. The guy gave Sam the creeps. Wayne always gave off the impression that he was trying to take advantage of the Ellerbys and, therefore, Sam, too.

After hours of research, Sam had learned quite a bit about Wayne: his upbringing, background, financial status, where he lived, pretty much everything there was to know about the guy.

It wasn't like Wayne was trying to hide or keep a low profile. Quite the opposite, in fact. Wayne Collins appeared to want attention and lots of it. Sam wasn't certain, but he had the feeling that was part of why Wayne was interested in discovering historical artifacts. He was in it for the thrill of the chase and the glory that came with finding something priceless. Based on the man's considerable fortune, he didn't need the money.

Another glance in the side mirror told Sam that Wayne and his partner were nowhere to be seen. Sam had a decent head start on the villains. At best, they would have been ten minutes behind, maybe five if they pushed it, but over the course of the drive, Sam hadn't seen any signs of the two troublemakers.

The kids remained silent during most of the journey. Sam figured they were reflecting on the dangerous events of the last few days. Maybe they were simply tired and catching up on some much-needed rest, though he didn't see any of them napping whenever he stole a quick look to the back seat. Billy, on the other hand, had passed out multiple times, probably still feeling the effects of the tranquilizer.

Sam shook his head. How could his partner have been so careless? Sam tried not to judge, but Billy letting those two knuckleheads get the better of him was something that shouldn't have happened.

Sam understood to a degree. They hadn't dealt with a real threat in a long time, more years than he could recall, in fact. Their job had become boring, and as a result, perhaps both of them had grown a tad soft.

That would change.

Sam had no intention of letting anyone get the drop on them again.

When they arrived in front of the hotel, he drove around the building in a full circle, all the way to the front where they found the valet. Billy and the kids climbed out, while Sam handed the keys to the young man in charge of parking cars. Sam eyed him for a second with a hint of suspicion in his eyes, and then walked away. He was just a kid, maybe eighteen or nineteen years old. No way was he a threat. Or was he? After the events from earlier in the day, it was hard to say anymore.

Sam shook off the paranoia and allowed the young man to take the car, slipping him a crisp bill before walking toward the door to join Billy and the kids.

The Ellerbys knew, to a degree, what was going on. Sam had Billy send them a few text messages on the way into the city so the couple wouldn't worry. While dinnertime was still a good twenty minutes away, the traffic, Billy explained, was what kept them from being back at the hotel sooner.

He wasn't lying. Billy also had no intention of telling the Ellerbys what really happened. There was no need to worry them with stories of two men who tried to steal something from their child and his friends.

The group walked into the hotel and made their way down the hallway. They reached the elevators and Desmond pressed one of the buttons. A ding came from the right, and a second later the doors opened. The kids stepped on board first, followed by the two men. Once the doors closed Sam looked down at the three kids.

"You all okay?"

The kids nodded. Diego yawned.

"Good. So, we're all in agreement about what to tell your parents, right?"

Desmond chuckled. "Yeah, we're all in the same boat now, aren't we?"

Sam rolled his eyes at the comment, but the kid wasn't wrong. They *were* all in the same boat, each having quite a bit to lose if the Ellerbys found out what they were up to.

"Remember, we're not lying to them. Understand. If they work you down to the point where you have to lie to keep from getting in trouble, then just be honest. We'll all have to swallow that pill together. That's part of the risk of doing what you...I mean, we're doing."

"Yeah, we won't tell them about those two bad guys," Corin said.

"Right," Diego agreed. "All we did was go to Sorano to check out the sights and visit an old museum."

Sam nodded. "Good. They should be fine with that."

"What are we going to tell them we're doing tomorrow?"

Sam grunted. He'd thought about that, but he didn't have an answer. "Well, we need to go see your friend the priest, right?"

The kids nodded as the elevator door opened. The kids started to step out into the hall, but Sam stopped them, blocking their path with his arm. He leaned his head out the opening and checked down the length of the corridor in both directions. It was empty. He pulled back his hand and motioned for the kids to proceed.

"Good. So, we tell them we're going to check out a cathedral and some other stuff in the city, maybe the Colosseum. I don't know. There's lots to do here."

"Yeah, you've mentioned that like a hundred times today." Desmond smirked.

Sam grinned. "Yeah, I have, haven't I?" He looked down at the kids. There was something about them. He'd been beyond irritated with them the day before, even earlier that morning. Now, though, he saw them in a different light. Sure, they'd been a bit mischievous sneaking into the vault and snooping around a ship that was part of a priceless, ancient collection. But they hadn't hurt anything. Well, there was a small piece of it they'd broken. Maybe no one would notice, or that's what they hoped.

The bodyguard didn't have an adventurous childhood. In fact, he didn't have much of a childhood at all. His parents were good to him. That wasn't the problem. The issue was that they were always on the go. Moving around from place to place didn't allow long-lasting friendships to form. It also kept him from getting close to anyone. Just when young Sam was starting to make friends, they would have to relocate again.

His parents gave him everything they could, supported him better than most, but he never developed strong bonds with other kids and thus never engaged in what some would call normal childhood fun, like running around the neighborhood, traipsing off into the woods, building tree houses, or finding buried treasure.

Was that what kids did?

Sam didn't know, but a part of him wanted Desmond and his friends to keep going. That part of him was the inner child that wanted to play pirates, go on adventures, and explore the world.

Then he snapped back to reality. Wayne and Carl were potentially dangerous. While they hadn't done anything to permanently hurt Billy, there was no telling what level those two would take their ambitions to. Sam's childhood desires for adventure and fun faded as his adult duty clouded over them. He had to protect the kids at all costs. Part of him wondered if letting them out of the building was a bad idea. The Ellerbys would be suspicious of that if they found out: not that the kids would tell.

Still, something pulled at Sam's heart. He wanted to know the truth. Was there really a treasure out there? He and Billy could take care of these three. That's what they were paid to do, and they were some of the best in the business. Or so they had thought. Billy getting caught earlier made Sam question that thought, but it was likely just luck. Sam would make sure that from now on luck would be on their side.

He escorted the three kids down the hall to their room and used his duplicate card key to unlock the door and let them in.

"Get cleaned up," Sam said in a professional tone. "Dinner is in twenty minutes. I'll be back to get you then. I don't want you having dinner while smelling like you've been on a farm for two weeks."

The kids smiled and nodded.

"Yes, sir," Corin said with a salute.

The boys said the same and hurried into the room to get ready.

Sam turned to Billy, who'd followed them down the corridor and was standing right behind him. He pulled his partner aside and ushered him toward their room a few doors down.

They stopped at the entrance, and Sam paused. He looked both directions as if he was about to share a deep secret.

"What's on your mind?" Billy asked. The haze was gone from his eyes, and he was fully alert now.

Sam rubbed his forehead with a finger and thumb. "Wayne and Carl. I don't know what they're going to do next."

"Yeah," Billy whispered. "Couple of bad eggs, those two."

"We need to think like they would. They may not be great archaeologists, but they were clever enough to track us to Sorano. That means they'll be thinking of another way to get to the kids."

"What do you think their next play will be?"

Sam shook his head. "Not sure. I'll have to consider it for a bit. If I was them, I know I'd be thinking about what we would be doing."

"Upping security. Making sure the hotel was secure. Probably even bringing in a few more people to watch the kids?"

"Yeah," Sam confirmed. "That's what we did do."

"It's gonna be tricky to keep the additional security people out of sight from the Ellerbys. They'll know something's up."

Sam nodded. "That is a problem. We'll need to request that the new people dress in plain clothes so as not to arouse suspicion. That should help. Position them in the lobby and outside the building like ordinary citizens and tourists. The Ellerbys are so busy with all this stuff going on around their exhibit, they won't pay any attention to whether or not the people they see in the building or on the streets are the same folks."

"That's a good start."

"Yeah. A good start." Sam knew that was all it really was. A start. He doubted Wayne and Carl would try to get into the building now, especially knowing what Sam's move would be.

The question was, how would they counter?

16

R ome

DINNER the previous night had been uneventful. But to Diego and Corin, the food was unlike anything they had ever tasted.

They'd been treated to a real Italian dinner with pasta made in-house, authentic sauces with fresh roasted garlic and newly pressed olive oil. The grilled zucchini and squash on the side was laced with rosemary and sea salt. Bread rolls with a crunchy crust and fluffy insides filled the room with bakery-like aromas. Then came the desserts. Chocolate gelato was the perfect way to end the meal, the creamy sweetness providing a delightful contrast to the salty, savory of the previous courses.

Desmond's parents had asked all the usual questions. They fell right into parent routine: How was your day? What did you guys do? See anything cool? Did you have fun?

They listened intently as the kids described the mountain town of

Sorano, the surroundings, the natural beauty, and how neat it was to see such an old and antiquated place so well preserved.

Both Ellerbys had been delighted that Sam and Billy were so willing to take the kids a few hours out of the city to see some unique historical sights.

At one point, Mr. Ellerby commended them both and thanked them, saying that it probably did the kids some good to get out of the chaotic city of Rome.

Sam ignored the kids beaming at him while at the same time dodging the temptation to tell them to look away or be more discreet. He did his best to flash them a subtle glance that would order the three to cool it, but the Ellerbys apparently didn't notice either.

Then there was the question about what they had planned for the following day.

Sam was surprised when the kids responded with a series of answers that all lent genuine credibility, without the need to be dishonest.

Mrs. Ellerby cautioned that they still had plenty of time to see most of Rome and beyond so not to press too hard to do it all in the first week.

"She's right," Sam had agreed quickly. "We have more than enough time to fill your minds with everything Rome has to offer."

The next morning, Sam and Billy woke up early as they always did. The night-shift guys would be ready to check out, eager to get some sleep. The partners took turns in the shower and then at the sink, throwing on deodorant and shaving, doing the things that middle-aged men did at that time of day.

When they were done, the two made their way out of the room and into the corridor. As the door closed behind them, a chill ran through Sam's veins. He stared toward the kids' room just two doors down. A startling and horrifying epiphany hit him. The night-shift guards were gone.

"Oh, no."

A million horrifying visions ran through Sam's head. Billy saw the problem a second later and started trotting toward the door.

"Where are they?" Billy asked.

"No idea. We traded off with them after dinner last night. They should be here."

Sam tapped a button on his radio. "Angel One to Angel Two, do you copy? What's your location?"

There was no response.

The surge of fear rushed through him again. Billy felt it, too. Panic wasn't something these two were accustomed to, but they were feeling it right now.

Sam ran his card over the surface of the locking mechanism on the kids' door and pushed it open when the light blinked green. Inside, the room was clean, the beds were made, and everything seemed normal. Everything except that there was no sign of the three children.

"Get on the horn with downstairs security," Sam ordered.

"Already on it," Billy said, putting the phone to his ear.

The two guards rushed out the door and down to the elevators. Luckily, one of the lifts happened to already be on their floor. Sam pressed the button, and the doors opened. It was empty.

The men stepped on, and Sam hit the button to the lobby. It only took thirty seconds for them to descend to the bottom. No one was answering the call from Billy's phone. He glanced, baffled, at Sam, wondering what to do next. Not many people were up this early in a hotel usually reserved for tourists, which meant no unnecessary stops along the way. The doors opened again when they reached the main floor, and the two men stepped out.

They scanned the room, frantic to find the night-shift guys. Suddenly, Sam spotted one of them standing over by the exit, chatting on his cell phone. Sam nearly sprinted across the room, ready to tackle the guy to find out what he was doing. Then he slowed down as his eye caught something off to the side.

Sitting at a round table, scarfing down pastries, fruits, and hot cocoa were Desmond, Diego, and Corin.

Sam scuffled to a stop and turned to face them. His face flushed red as he caught his breath and flattened his suit jacket. Billy caught up a second later and upon seeing the three kids, hit the end button on his phone and shoved it back into a pocket.

"What are you three doing?" Sam tried not to sound angry or mean, but he was frustrated. In his line of work, things needed to go a certain way, every time, all the time. Unplanned events or sudden decisions usually ended in trouble. He'd seen it cause even the best-laid plans to unravel quickly.

"Eating breakfast," Desmond said with a full mouth. He shrugged, wondering what the problem was.

Sam's eyes darted to one of the night-shift guys standing by the counter, getting a cup of coffee. He didn't know how those types did it. They were a different breed. They worked weird hours and then drank coffee in the morning like everyone else, except for them; it was like a final ritual before heading to bed. Sam then looked at the guy by the doors, still talking on his phone.

They were, apparently, unconcerned.

"You didn't see anyone suspicious, did you?" Sam asked.

The three kids shook their heads.

Corin washed down a pastry with a swig of water. "No. The other guards are nice, but they're kind of quiet. They've been watching out for trouble."

She was an astute young lady; that much was evident. Sam had never seen kids this age with such a sense for things like that. Then again, he already knew there was something special about them. They were, after all, trying to figure out a two-thousand-year-old Roman mystery. And they were getting close to solving it. Impressive for anyone their age.

"You wanna have a seat?" Diego asked. "We got some extra food for you and Mr. Billy."

Billy's eyebrows knit together, and his eyes welled. He didn't have to be invited twice. "That is the nicest thing anyone has done for me in a long time."

He pulled up a chair and sat down next to Diego, snatching one of the sugary pastries before looking up at his partner's glare. It wasn't disapproving, more like a curious stare, one a person would give if they saw a purple monkey.

"Just call me Billy," the guard said with a full mouth. A crumb dribbled from the corner of his lips, over his chin, and onto the table.

The kids watched the man scarf down his food. They had been raised better than to eat like that.

"Have a seat, Mr. Sam," Diego offered with a pleasant smile.

Sam panned the room, his eyes darting from one side to the other without so much as a twitch from his head. "Thanks. I will in a second. I need to talk to the night-shift guys first."

He walked over to the guard at the coffee counter and stood next to him as he waited for his order to be delivered.

"What are you guys doing, Todd?" Sam asked.

Todd was athletic but slimmer and shorter than Sam. Sam knew the guy had fighting skills. Based on Todd's wiry frame, Sam guessed some kind of Brazilian jujitsu. Maybe boxing.

"Shift's over in five minutes," the man said, rechecking his watch. "Kids wanted some breakfast, so we brought them down to eat. Never seen kids so eager to get up early and start the day."

Sam ignored much of the statement. "Perimeter check?"

"Clean," Todd said. "No sign of trouble." Then he looked around the lobby as if about to ask an extremely personal question. "What's going on, Sam? You seem spooked. You never seem spooked."

Sam did his best to put on a calm, nonchalant expression. "Nothing. It's nothing."

Todd shook his head. "See, I know you're lying. People are lying when they repeat themselves the way you just did."

The barista set the guard's coffee on the counter next to an everything bagel.

"I'm not lying. Everything's good," Sam insisted.

"Something got you spooked. You don't get that look easily. Now you're down here all worried about the kids eating breakfast in the lobby." He took a plastic knife and spread some cream cheese on one side of his bagel. "That tells me something happened, probably yesterday. And the men you told us to watch for, the Wayne and Carl characters, that's awfully specific, too, Sam."

He finished the job with the cream cheese and mashed the two halves of bagel together. Then he picked up his coffee and the little white plate and moved over to one of the nearby standing tables, just far enough out of earshot from the kids.

Sam followed him, albeit reluctantly. He disliked being told what to do almost as much as he disliked shoddy protocol and slacking on the job.

Todd put his food and drink on the table. Then he picked up the mug and drew a sip. After a satisfied "ah" he put it back down and looked Sam squarely in the eyes.

"Way I see it, those kids got into some kind of trouble yesterday. I'm not sure what it has to do with Wayne Collins, but you don't have to worry about it, Sam. We'll take care of them. Just like you and Billy do on your shift." He took a small bite of the bagel, chewed for a second, and went on. "I'm just saying it's sketchy. Wayne Collins is sketchy. If you've got us and the two new guys outside watching for them, something is up."

Sam thought long and hard about it. Honesty was something he'd always valued. A million lies ran through his head. He couldn't tell Todd about the treasure, not because he didn't trust the guy, but because that would lead to more questions, maybe even deeper involvement. Then there was the issue that it could be brought up with the Ellerbys. The fewer people who knew about the treasure and the map, the better.

"We think Wayne and his partner are planning something big."

Todd raised one eyebrow and took another sip of coffee. "Something big? What do you mean? Like a crime?"

Sam nodded. "Yeah."

"Like I said before, those two always came off as shady to me. I had a feeling it would only be a matter of time before they tried something stupid. What are they up to?"

Sam had already figured out how to word everything. "We think they tampered with the video surveillance system the other night at the gala."

"Really?"

Sam nodded. "Yep. For about thirty minutes or so, the feed was looped. Intentionally. We know because we went back through the recordings and looked at times we knew different people were there." He omitted the part about the kids snooping around in the vault. Todd didn't need to know who was in the area, just that someone was. "Then we saw them yesterday skulking around. They followed us to Sorano."

A look of grave concern washed over Todd's face. "Followed you? Why would they do that?"

Sam rolled his shoulders. "Maybe they were planning on stealing something from the exhibit and got spooked, then came back around thinking a better plan would be to nab the kids and use them—"

"For a ransom," Todd finished the sentence.

Sam let him believe that. "Whatever it is, we need to keep a close eye on this place until the Ellerbys and their guests return to the States. Understood?"

Todd nodded. "I'm still a bit surprised that Wayne is resorting to crime now. Why? He doesn't need the money."

"Some people don't care about money," Sam said. "They're more interested in power and fame. Wayne has some influence back in the UK. And like you said, he has money. That leaves only one thing that he doesn't have."

"Fame?"

"Yeah."

"Seems a little thin to me." Todd rolled his shoulders and took another sip of coffee.

"Maybe. Or maybe if you had the right motivation, the right background and upbringing, that could be a combination buried deep down that would drive someone to do whatever he's doing."

"Yeah." Todd's head bobbed up and down. "But if he stole something from the bosses, they'd know about it. It's not like he could put it out there for all the world to see, showing it off and all that like it was his discovery."

Todd was right. Sam knew that much. That could mean only one thing: Wayne's initial plan had been revenge. Steal something from the vault because he'd never been as big as the Ellerbys in the eyes of the archaeological and scientific communities. Revenge. It was always a top-three motive when crime was involved. It made perfect sense.

Sam was satisfied with his conclusion, but it also brought up another issue. If Wayne was set on revenge and failed with his first attempt, how far would he take the next one?

He thanked Todd and told him and his partner they were relieved for the rest of the day. Todd checked his watch and nodded, returning to his steaming cup of coffee.

Sam walked back over to the table where the kids and Billy were finishing breakfast. He put on his best fake smile and pulled up a chair. "Mind if I join you?"

The kids grinned. Sam could tell they were warming to him. That made him feel good, though he did his best to keep emotions aside. Through the years, Desmond had become like a little brother to him, maybe even a son in some ways. Sam sensed that same sentiment growing rapidly for Desmond's friends, too. They were in his charge, and it was up to him to take care of them.

"So," Sam said, "we're going to the museum. Then the church. Yeah?"

He picked up a crusty roll and a slice of cheese. His teeth cut through the bread, and after a few seconds of chewing, he took a bite of cheese, too.

The kids nodded.

"Yeah, if that's okay with you." Desmond looked hopeful.

"Hey," Sam replied with a mouthful of food, "we already discussed it. That's the plan." Then he leaned in close. "But we have to be careful, okay? I don't want anything like what happened yesterday happening again. Those two are dangerous, and they're still out there. We'll keep our eyes open, but you need to as well. Okay?"

The kids nodded their agreement.

"Good."

He looked out the window at the people walking on the sidewalk, noting the cars buzzing by just beyond.

The sooner he could get the Ellerbys and these kids out of Italy, the sooner he'd feel a lot better about this whole situation.

17

R ome

THE MUSEUM CURATOR who was on duty was more than happy to help the Ellerbys' son and his friends. The second Sam mentioned their names, the skinny Italian man's eyes widened, and he couldn't nod enough in agreement to their requisition.

"Ah, Desmond Ellerby," he'd said. "I'm sorry I didn't meet you the other night at the gala."

Desmond had blown off the fact, hoping to avoid the truth about their mischief that took them into the vault and onto the boat.

The curator, a man named Paolo, escorted them into one of the secure hallways. The kids raised collective eyebrows as they strode by the vault where the ship was still being studied and worked on by the research team.

Diego bit his lip, thinking for a second that simply being close to that room again would implicate them.

At the end of the hall, they turned left into another open door and found themselves in a huge lab. Empty beakers rested on top of metal tables to the right. Fragments of papyrus were strewn across the surface of one in the center. Tools like tweezers, spatulas, brushes, and tongs hung from the wall to the left.

In the back corner of the room sat the device they'd come to use. The CR-10 3-D printer wasn't top-of-the-line technology, but for their purposes it would do the job.

"It's right back here," Paolo said, extending a bony finger at the machine.

He ushered them across the room to the machine and pulled out a few chairs so two of the guests could sit.

"I'll get a few more seats for you."

"I'm fine, thank you," Sam said.

"Me, too," Diego added, trying to sound tough.

Desmond and Corin slid into the chairs and waited for the curator to turn on the printer and run through a short checklist of preparations. Then he switched on the desktop next to the printer and logged in.

"What kind of design software do you have?" Corin asked.

Paolo grinned and clicked on an application. "Fusion," he said. "It's the best one on the market right now."

"Oh, yeah. That is a good one."

"You know how to use it?" he asked.

She nodded. "I've dabbled in it before but never actually been able to print anything with it."

"She's really good," Diego said. "I like to draw characters for stories and comic books. She designs them on the computer. Maybe someday we'll have a printer of our own we can use to make them."

"Sounds fun," Paolo said. His accent was heavy, but he spoke perfect English. Sam wondered if the man had been educated in an English-speaking country or perhaps a school with native speakers.

"Doesn't sound like you need me for this part of it, then," Paolo said. "I'll leave you to it. When you're ready to print, just let me know, and I'll come back and take care of all of the pre-print settings. How big is the object you're wanting to create?"

Corin showed him the pictures she took while Desmond used his hands to emulate how large the object would be.

"Oh, our printer can handle something that size." Paolo cocked his head to the side and continued staring at the pictures. "That's an interesting rock. Looks like it says something on it."

"Yeah," Corin said in an unsteady voice. "We don't really know what that is. Probably some teenager who thought it would be cool to carve their name on it." She quickly closed her phone's screen, trying not to be too obvious.

"Well, have fun. I'll be in my office when you're ready to make this...thing. Here's my number." He wrote down the phone number and extension where he could be reached, then pointed at a phone on the end of the table. "You can use that over there if your cell phones don't have service here. Actually, it might be better if you use it since I don't answer calls from unknown numbers."

"Thanks, Paolo," Sam said. "We appreciate the help."

"For the Ellerbys, anything I can do is a pleasure."

The man took a bow and excused himself, walking back out the only door in and out of the lab.

Corin and the kids returned their attention to the computer as she used a USB cord next to the monitor to connect the desktop to her phone. It took only a second before a new application appeared on the screen, displaying her device and asking if she'd like to import photos and videos.

She clicked a few buttons, and the images of the keystone appeared.

Sam took a step back and looked toward the open door. He didn't hear anything unusual coming from the corridor just beyond, but he wanted to make sure. He walked over to the doorway and poked his head outside. Paolo was already gone, probably to the lobby or back in his office.

He pressed the button on his earpiece. "How's it looking out there, Billy?"

"All clear, chief," Billy said.

They'd made the decision to keep their usual procedure in

place. Billy would stay outside and keep an eye on things. Sam wished they had another person or two. There was a lot to watch out there, but Billy could handle it. There were multiple points of entry, but he was confident museum security wouldn't allow another breach.

"Thanks," Sam said.

"You bet."

Sam turned and strode back over to the workstation. Corin was clicking the mouse rapidly, expanding a two-dimensional image on the screen into 3-D. His eyebrows lowered and his face drew into a confused frown.

"How do you do that?" He wasn't stupid, but there were some things in the tech world he didn't understand. This was one of them.

"It's 3-D modeling software," Corin explained. "You can take a flat image and make it three dimensional. See?" She clicked on a few things, and then one side of the stone expanded. Then she clicked two more times on a couple of items from a dropdown menu, and the keystone rotated on the screen. "I'll just be a few more minutes and then we can call Paolo."

Sam chuckled. "I think he was expecting this to take a bit longer."

"Well," Desmond chimed in, "the print itself will take a long time. Could be as much as two or three hours. The model is pretty simple, so maybe that will cut down on the time."

"Plus, I don't have to have it on super detailed settings," Corin added. "I'll limit the resolution somewhat so the machine will print faster. It's just a piece of rock, so there isn't a ton of detail except for the letters."

"Two or three hours?" Sam sounded concerned about this revelation. "What are we going to do for three hours?"

Corin rolled her shoulders. "I don't know. Wait?"

"That's going to be a boring three hours for you, isn't it?"

"Honestly, I didn't really think about that before we got here. Maybe we can have the curator lock the door so we can go check out some of the sights near here."

"Good idea," Diego said. "If those two guys are still out there and they're following us, we might be able to throw them off by checking out some random historical places."

"Yeah," Desmond agreed.

Sam had to admit these kids were clever, although he didn't like the insinuation that they were making. If Wayne and Carl were following them, and Diego was suggesting they lead the two astray, it was effectively using the kids as bait.

"It's not a horrible idea," Sam said. "And I like where your head's at."

Diego gave an appreciative nod.

"But I also don't like the idea of luring those two toward us."

"Well, then we sit here and wait for the next few hours until the print is done," Corin said.

Sam knew the kids would be bored out of their minds just sitting there in a lab for that amount of time. They'd get restless, want to start wandering around or playing with things they shouldn't. At least that was his experience with children in boring settings.

"No, you know what? I like it. Let's head out to the Colosseum and see if we can get in with one of their tours. It's still early, so I doubt they've filled up yet. We'll come back here in a couple of hours and get the model."

"And from there we'll head back to see our priest," Desmond finished the thought.

"Right," Sam said with a nod. "Okay, let's call the curator and get him back over here to set this thing up."

He walked over to the phone and dialed the extension from memory. The friendly Italian answered after two rings.

"Hey, Paolo, it's Sam with the kids in the lab. We're ready to print this thing."

18

R ome

PAOLO MADE his final adjustments to the printer settings using a round metal knob on the front of the control box. The blue LED display made an electronic ding every time he selected a particular item from the menu. It was kind of annoying, but the kids didn't care. They were fascinated by the technology. On more than one occasion, Desmond mentioned getting this particular model for his workspace back home in the States.

Once Paolo was done, he hit the knob and twisted it a few more times, pressed it again, and then the printer hummed to life. The extruder slid back and forth over the print bed as it began squeezing the melted filament out onto the surface in thin, almost undetectable layers.

"Looks like the print time will be just over two hours," Paolo said. "Would take longer if we hadn't adjusted the settings."

Corin nodded knowingly and flashed a wink at her friends.

"I don't know what you all have planned, but you're welcome to hang around here or take a tour of the museum."

The kids had already seen most of the museum, not to mention the restricted area.

"I think I'm going to take them to see the Colosseum," Sam cut in. "Right, kids?"

They all nodded together.

"Yeah," Desmond said. "I've been wanting to check that out since we got here." He wasn't lying. The Colosseum was at the top of all their lists of things to see and do while in Rome.

"Excellent," Paolo said. "I'm sure you'll enjoy it."

"Is there any way we can lock that door over there?" Sam asked, pointing at the only way in and out.

"Lock it? Certainly. Why?"

Sam shrugged and pulled the curator aside, as if about to share top-secret information with him. "The kids don't want whatever they're making to be stolen. I know you have a secure area here, but could you do it for me?"

Paolo saw the pleading in Sam's eyes. "Absolutely. Not a problem, Sam. Like I said before, I'm always happy to help."

"Thank you."

Sam followed the kids out of the lab and down the hall while Paolo remained behind to lock up. The bodyguard gave one last look over his shoulder as he and the kids passed through the door and out into the lobby. He touched his radio again to hail Billy.

"Hey, we're coming out. Need to give the printer a few hours to make this thing."

"Ten-four, chief. So, what's the plan?"

"We're going to head over to the Colosseum, maybe take a tour."

"Awesome. I've always wanted to go there." Billy didn't try to hide the childlike excitement in his voice or the hope that hung with it.

Sam caught what his partner was getting at. Billy didn't want to be stuck waiting outside again. Lucky for him, Sam wasn't going to ask Billy to do that. With a place as big and crowded as the Colosseum, it would be impossible to monitor anything suspicious outside. There would be too many people, cars, and distractions. Besides, Sam had a feeling that snaked through his gut. It was a sense he'd had many times before when danger was near. If something went down and Wayne and Carl tried anything, Sam wanted to make sure he and Billy were close by to have each other's backs. A little extra protection never hurt.

"Glad to hear it," Sam said. "I've kind of always wondered what the fuss was about with that place, too. I guess I'll find out today."

"Cool. I'll have the car ready out front."

They passed through the cavernous lobby, walking by the prominent display cases, works of art hanging on the walls, and the information desk where a young woman with curly brown hair was busily working on her computer.

Corin stopped at the sound of her phone. It had just hit her that no one had even reached out to her or Diego since they had arrived, making her wonder who it might be.

Sliding the device out of her jean pocket, Corin caught sight of the caller ID: it was her mother.

"Hey, Sam!" Corin called ahead, watching as the bodyguard turned to see what he was being called for. "My mom is calling. Give me a minute?"

"I wanna talk, too!" Diego beamed at the thought of talking to his parents again.

"Hey, Mom!"

"Corin! It seems like it's been forever! How is Rome? Are you having fun?" Her mom wasted no time before spewing questions at her daughter.

"It's a blast! There are so many cool things here. We even—" Corin stopped herself from spilling the secret of the keystones. She knew if her parents found out about Wayne and Carl chasing them for a treasure, they would immediately be sent back home. There was no way Corin was going to let that happen.

"What did you do?" Her mom asked, eagerly wondering what it was.

"We even got to see an old cathedral!" Diego jumped in on the conversation, snatching the phone from his sister.

"That's really cool, and it's great to hear from you too, Diego!" Diego flashed a smile at the excitement in his mom's voice.

"Well, we're off to the Colosseum right now, so we will call you later."

"All right. You two be safe."

"Always," Corin added, ending the call and putting it back into her pocket.

"Ready?" Sam asked, waiting patiently with Desmond.

"Yup!" The two said simultaneously.

Once outside, a burst of warm air splashed over them and stripped away the comfort of the museum's cool interior. The smells of Rome filled their nostrils once more: the exhaust from vehicles, coffee brewing in a nearby café, bread baking, garlic sautéing.

Billy pulled the SUV up to the curb and the kids climbed into the back. Sam hopped in the front, and they took off, merging into the chaos once more.

When the group arrived at the Colosseum, Billy had some trouble finding a parking space. People, mostly tourists, were everywhere, milling about in front of the gates to the Colosseum, likely waiting on their guided tours to begin.

The visitors were from all walks of life, countries, and ethnic backgrounds. The hodgepodge of tourists all had one thing in common, however: they were mesmerized by the massive ancient arena.

To a person, every head craned up at the walls towering above them. They admired the arched portals that served as windows into the past. While some of the sections appeared to be crumbling, most of the Colosseum was in amazing shape considering its age. It had been refurbished and renovated a few times to keep its structural integrity, but simply being next to it truly felt like going back in time by thousands of years.

The second the kids got out of the car, they mirrored all the other visitors staring up at the Colosseum with wide-eyed wonder.

"Over there," Billy said, pointing a thick index finger at the ticket booth near one of the gates.

The group made their way through the gathering crowd. They walked by a group of Japanese tourists, the guide prattling on in their language about what surely must have been facts, historical tidbits, and legends about the Colosseum. That cacophony was amplified by similar groups, and their own tour guides, from South America, Africa, and Eastern Europe.

"It's amazing how many multilingual tour guides they have here," Sam said.

They passed another group with a blond man with wire-rimmed glasses speaking German.

"That's a cool job," Diego said. "Would be fun to do something like that, getting to walk around a historic place like this all the time."

"For sure," Desmond agreed.

After snaking their way through the masses, they got in line for tickets. As they waited, the kids continued to gaze up at the building, still in awe at the scope of it.

Sam and Billy, on the other hand, were busy scanning the crowd. They appreciated the historical significance and amazing architectural imagination that went into creating the Colosseum, but they had pressing things to worry about. Out here, surrounded by so many people, it could be extremely easy to lose track of one of the kids.

Sam started thinking maybe this had been a bad idea, but it was too late to turn back now. The kids had their hearts set on seeing this landmark. He could see it in their eyes. For these three history buffs, it may as well have been Christmas morning. Sam sighed and kept looking around, shuffling forward as the patrons in front of them paid for their tickets and stepped out of line.

Once they reached the sales window, Sam asked for five tickets and handed the dark-haired woman inside the booth a fistful of euros. He clutched the tickets and motioned for the kids and Billy to step away from the booth even as he took another quick look around.

He handed one to each person and then crossed his arms, putting on his best stern face so the kids would know he was being serious.

The three friends were about to explode from excitement.

"Okay, settle down for a second, you three." Sam kept his poker face so they wouldn't think he was fooling around.

Corin bit her bottom lip. Desmond was grinning from ear to ear. Diego just stood on his toes like he was about to blast off.

"Now," Sam began, "we're in a very crowded place, okay?"

They nodded.

"That means it's real easy for us to get separated if you three don't pay close attention. Don't wander off. Stay close to me and Billy. I know you're all excited to be here and you can't get in there fast enough, but try to contain yourselves."

He couldn't believe how visiting a historic monument was making these kids so antsy. When he was a kid, growing up in the 1980s, all he wanted to do was play video games or baseball. Clearly, this Adventure Guild enjoyed more scholarly pursuits.

"I don't want to have another run-in with Wayne and his crony. It's possible they followed us here, which is fine. They won't be stupid enough to try anything with so many people around. That said, don't wander off." He felt the need to repeat that last part. "Billy and I are pumped up about taking a tour through this place as well. Now, the ticket lady said our tour will begin over there." He pointed at a spot about thirty feet from the front gate. "We have about ten minutes to kill before we go inside. You need to do anything: food, drink, whatever before we go?"

The kids collectively shook their heads.

"No?" Sam shrugged. "Okay. Stay close to the group," he said it one more time. "And especially to me and Billy."

They nodded again, and then Billy led the way over to the spot where they would rendezvous with their guided group. Sam kept an eye on the three kids to make sure they didn't get separated, but he also kept his head on a swivel, turning it one way and then the other, panning the mobs of people for a familiar face he hoped wouldn't be there.

Sam knew it was going to be a long day of keeping watch over the course of the next several hours. Being out in the open like this made him feel exposed. He suddenly pined for the safety of the museum, the comfort of being in a building with walls and corners, doors where you could see who was coming.

The bright sun beat down from a perfect azure sky. He loosened his tie against the heat and swallowed. He let out a long sigh from his nose and bit his lower lip. Yeah, it was going to be a long day.

19

Rome

SAM OPENED the door to the museum and held it wide for the three kids to walk in. Billy stepped on the gas and whipped the SUV around the corner to park it on the side of the building.

The kids' voices echoed through the museum lobby as they chattered about things they'd seen, facts they'd learned, and the overall incredible experience of touring the Colosseum.

Sam let the door close behind him as he followed the three friends across the shiny tiled floor toward the information desk. It had been an amazing day, and Sam couldn't hide the smile from his face. He felt like a proud father with the three kids.

He also felt an overwhelming sense of relief flood over him as he stepped farther into the museum atrium.

Nothing had happened while they were at the Colosseum, though more than a few times he'd snapped his head around at a suspicious pop or a kid screaming. Each time, it had turned out to be nothing, but that hadn't kept him from being on edge during the entirety of the tour.

Now that they were back, he was much more at ease, although never fully relaxed. Relaxation would have to wait until he was on a beach back in the States.

He approached the information desk and frowned, his forehead wrinkling as confusion seeped into his mind. Where was the woman who usually worked here?

Sam stopped at the façade in front of her desk and leaned over. There was no sign of her. "That's odd," he said.

The three kids stood close behind him, all eager to get back to the lab and check out the 3-D print of the keystone.

"What?" Corin asked, taking a step closer to the counter.

"The girl that works here at the info desk. No sign of her."

Sam turned around and looked up to the second and third tiers of the museum. The wraparound walkways above were empty. He wasn't surprised that no tourists were there. The building was closed for the week while teams of people worked to get it ready to display all the artifacts from the Ellerby discovery.

The workers and research teams were likely back in the vault. Still, the place was quiet. Too quiet.

"What's wrong?" Diego asked, looking up at the bodyguard with sincere curiosity.

"Nothing, Diego. Nothing. Let's go take a look at that model you guys made. I'm sure the reception lady is around here somewhere."

Sam led the three friends over to the secure access door and entered the code he'd been given at the beginning of the week. The door clicked, and he pulled it open, allowing the kids to walk through first.

He let the door close behind him as they headed down the corridor. A twinge of relief trickled through his veins as he glanced into the vault and saw dozens of people working tirelessly on several different pieces for the exhibit.

Okay, Sam thought. *That's more like it.*

Seeing the workers took a load off his mind and relieved him of the paranoia that was beating his brain.

They continued down the hall and reached the door but found it was closed. Sam recalled asking Paolo to lock the lab so no one would mess with what they were doing on the 3-D printer. Desmond checked the door handle. Giving it a tug, he confirmed it was locked.

"You know where the curator is?" Corin asked.

"No," Sam said with a shake of the head. "I can call him, though." He pulled out his cell phone and dialed the number from memory.

Diego's face tightened into a frown. "You remembered that number from earlier?"

Sam answered with a nod as he listened to the phone ring on the other end. After several seconds of waiting, Paolo's voice mail picked up.

Sam ended the call and scowled. Something wasn't right.

He stepped between the kids and grasped the handle, jerking it down. Again, the door didn't budge.

"Didn't you see what I just did?" Desmond asked.

"Yeah, sorry. Always good to double check."

Sam leaned to the right, nearly to the point where his right cheek pressed against the square glass window in the middle of the door. He could see the tables in the center of the room. Beyond that, he could make out the back corner where the 3-D printer sat idly.

He squinted, trying to get a better view of something he thought he saw on the floor. Then, his eyes abruptly widened. "Oh, no."

Sam grabbed the handle again and shook it.

"What's wrong?" Desmond asked. "I told you, it's locked."

"I think the curator is in there."

He looked back down the hall, suddenly concerned for the kids' safety.

Sam put out his arm and herded the three into the back corner, opposite the door into the lab. He blinked rapidly, trying to think of what to do, while making sure no one could get the drop on them.

If Paolo was in the lab and on the floor, he needed help.

Sam eyed the keypad next to the door and made a quick decision.

Maybe the code he'd been given would open this door, too. It was worth a shot.

He stepped to the pad and entered his code. There was an electric buzz followed by a click.

Relief flooded over Sam as he grabbed the handle again and pulled it down. This time, the door came free and swung open into the lab. Sam stepped inside and held a palm up for the kids to wait there.

"Billy? I need you to get in here right away."

"Copy that, chief. On my way."

"We're in the hallway that leads to the vault and the lab. I'm going into the lab now. Something has happened."

As he stepped farther into the room, he saw two sets of legs poking out from behind the other side of the table. One pair of legs wore dark pantyhose and were attached to black high heels. The other pair was covered in the same slacks Paolo had been wearing earlier.

Sam reached into his holster and pulled out a pistol. He didn't want to do that in front of the kids, but now he had no choice.

He held the weapon out with both hands on the grip and a finger tense on the trigger. He swept the room, checking every possible hiding spot before moving deeper.

"Stay there," Sam ordered without looking over his shoulder. He sensed the kids' urge to follow him into the room, but if it came to firing his weapon, he'd prefer they be out in the hall where stray rounds couldn't find them.

He heard footsteps clicking in the corridor, hurrying his way.

Sam pressed the button. "That you coming?"

"Yeah."

"Stay out there with the kids. I'm checking the lab now."

Billy didn't need to ask his partner why he was sweeping the lab. They had an understanding. When Billy heard that tone in Sam's voice, he knew something was up. They'd worked together for years, and that chemistry had evolved organically over time.

Sam crept around the end of the table and took inventory of every possible hiding place. He looked back over the table at the other work areas. No one else was in here; of that he was certain.

He stuffed his pistol back into his holster and rushed to the other end of the table. Before he reached the back-right corner, he saw what had happened to Paolo and the receptionist.

They were tied together with duct tape around their waists, gagged with the same tape over their mouths, and bound at the wrists and ankles, too.

Sam reached into a pocket and pulled out a small knife. He opened the blade and started working the tape binding the two together. They made muffled noises and wiggled, their voices rising in muted panic.

"Stay still," Sam said.

"You okay in there, Sam?" Billy's voice echoed in the sterile room.

"Yeah. Stay out there for a second."

The knife sliced through the duct tape and freed the two from each other. Then he made quick work of the bonds around their ankles and wrists, saving their mouths for last since it would take a much more careful touch.

When the young woman was completely free, she gasped for air, relieved to finally be breathing through her mouth and nose again.

"Thank you," she said. Tears welled in her eyes. "Those men. They came in and..." Her voice faded as she started crying.

"It's okay," Sam said. "You're fine. Here." He pulled up a nearby chair. "Sit down."

She did as instructed and slumped into the seat.

"What happened, Paolo?" Sam asked, turning to the curator.

Paolo rubbed his wrists to get the circulation back into his fingers. "I don't know," he said. "I was in my office working, and two men came in. They were wearing sunglasses and hats. I thought that was weird. They had a gun and told me to get up, then ordered me to accompany them down here. When I stepped out of my office, I realized they had Giulia." He motioned to the young woman.

"What did they want? Who was it?"

Paolo shook his head. "They forced us down here and made me

unlock the lab. They...they wanted your 3-D object, but I don't know why. I told them it was just something the kids were working on."

Sam's eyes widened. "They took the print?"

Paolo nodded.

The kids entered the room as the curator relayed the information to Sam.

"Wait," Corin interrupted. "What did you just say?"

Sam turned to face the kids as they rushed across the floor to where Sam was standing near the printer.

"They took the print version of the keystone," he said.

"Who did?" Paolo asked. "Who were those people?"

Sam knew. The kids knew, too.

"Wayne Collins and his sidekick, Carl." The bodyguard could see the names didn't ring a bell so he gave a quick explanation of how Wayne was a failed treasure hunter, jealous of the Ellerbys and their success.

Corin, Diego, and Desmond sagged. Disappointment flooded their faces the same way it would if they woke up to a lump of coal in their stockings on December 25.

"Oh, no," Diego said. "What do we do?"

"I say we go after them," Desmond suggested. "They couldn't have gotten far."

"They left more than an hour ago," Paolo stated. "They're long gone by now." He paused to reflect for a moment. "What was so important about that print you three made?"

Desmond sighed. He was about to answer when Sam did it for him.

"It's something they've been working on, and I'm helping them. We think it could lead to an important historical discovery."

Paolo chuckled until he saw the bodyguard wasn't kidding. "Really? What is it?"

"That's not important right now. What's important is that you're all safe." He turned back to the kids. "No, we aren't going after Wayne and Carl. It's too dangerous."

"We can't just give up," Corin said. "We've come this far, too far to give up now."

Sam nodded. "I know. We're not giving up. Those two have crossed a line twice now."

"But that guy just said they're long gone." Diego pointed at Paolo.

"Sure," Sam said. "But we still have the printer and Corin's phone. We can use it to make another keystone."

"I'm sorry. Keystone?" Paolo injected.

"Yes," Sam didn't even look at the skinny Italian this time. "We can run another print, go to the church, and ask your friend for help."

"Church?" Paolo interrupted again.

"There's a priest there who speaks Latin," Sam said. "There's something on that keystone that's engraved in Latin. We need the priest to translate for us."

"Why not just ask the Ellerbys to do that? Desmond's parents speak Latin."

Sam sighed and looked over at the curator again. "Let's just say we'd prefer to keep this little project a secret from them. Capisci?"

Paolo pouted his lower lip and rolled his shoulders. "Well, if you're in a hurry and need to keep it a secret, I can help."

Billy jumped into the conversation after having stood there for minutes in total silence. "How can you help?"

"I speak Latin."

Corin plugged her phone into the desktop before she remembered the images were probably still on the machine. She checked the folders on the screen and found the recent imports. Sure enough, the images she'd put on there earlier in the day were still intact. Paolo busily worked on the printer settings to make sure everything was ready and in place.

She finished checking the 3-D renderings and then stood aside so Paolo could do his thing. He turned a knob, pressed it, turned it again, and then the machine hummed to life.

"No time to worry about getting too detailed with this one," Paolo said.

The printer's extruder started moving back and forth as it poured the melted plastic onto the glass build surface.

"What do we do now?" Diego asked.

"Once this thing is done, we make our next move. I'd wager Wayne and Carl found someone to translate the inscription for them, but that doesn't mean they have the riddle figured out yet. There may still be time for us to beat them to it."

"Beat them to what?" Paolo looked genuinely curious.

"Caesar's Secret."

THANK YOU

We just want to say thank you for continuing this adventure with the kids from the Adventure Guild.

Be sure to check out the exciting conclusion of the *Caesar Secret* in book 3 of this trilogy.

We know that you could spend your time and money on other books. There are millions of them out there, but you chose to hang out with us for a while in this fun adventure. We appreciate that.

Be sure to join the Adventure Guild to get exclusive content, interviews, and some cool swag reserved for members only.

Thanks again for reading.

Chandler and Ernest

<<<<>>>>

JOIN THE GUILD

I f you enjoyed this story, be sure to join The Adventure Guild to get updates on upcoming releases and exclusive content. You'll also get sneak peaks at future chapters before anyone else! Join here.

OTHER BOOKS IN THE SERIES

The Caesar Secret Part 1

Made in the USA
Monee, IL
21 October 2021

80561886R10083